KEEPING THE BOOKS

Developing
Financial Capacity
in Your
Nonprofit Press

♦

THE STEVENS GROUP

This financial resource manual highlights several legal and tax-related issues affecting nonprofit organizations. The information presented is meant to serve as a general guideline only and is not a substitute for legal advice. In all situations involving local, state or federal law, obtain specific and current information from the appropriate government agency or from a qualified professional.

Keeping the Books: Developing Financial Capacity in Your Nonprofit Press

Request additional copies by contacting:
The Stevens Group, 570 Asbury Street, Suite 207, St. Paul, MN 55104

Authors: Susan Kenny Stevens, Lisa M. Anderson and Eric P. Stoebner, CPA

Cover illustration and design by MacLean & Tuminelly
Production and design by Brenda Christoffer, The Stevens Group
Printed by Thomson-Shore, Inc.

Edited by Bartels-Rabb Communications

Published by

THE STEVENS GROUP
FINANCIAL MANAGEMENT CONSULTANTS

First Edition

Printed in the United States of America

ISBN 0-9652208-6-9

table of contents

preface

Notes From a Cash Guy Trapped in an Accrual World

— Scott Walker

Beginnings

Starting a small publishing company takes an angel's combination of idealism, passion, unreasonableness, innocence, naiveté and blind obedience to an inner voice telling you to go heart- and head-long into something utterly likely to fail. It would in fact be a kindness if the venture failed, because success requires so much time and intellectual and emotional energy that it squeezes to death every last healthy impulse you had to start with.

To keep going as a publisher requires luck and a mundane assortment of personality defects. It helps enormously if you have nothing better to do, are out of touch with your feelings (agony, worry, exhaustion, frustration . . .) and are disinclined to concentrate on any one thing for more than a few minutes at a time. (These faults are more often referred to as commitment, bravery and an ability to do a lot of things at once. This is clearly propaganda.) Keeping a press going also takes a rat-in-a-maze ability to learn from mistakes, ask for and listen to advice and then discern which advice is best ignored.

When the two original wolves launched Graywolf Press in 1974, we had in mind a vision that could have been summarized in a one-sentence "mission statement," if we'd known what a mission statement was. We wanted to publish good writing beautifully. Our respect for and involvement in contemporary literature was matched with our love for beautiful and well-made books. Our innocence cannot be underestimated; it is as if there existed in our minds two unarticulated ideals, called "writing" and "beautiful book," toward which we were driven, and as if we were forced to utter them in a foreign language. We used the word "publish" without quite realizing what it meant. And we were years away from understanding that we were making an organization as well as books. That we were making a business never occurred to us.

Innocence and naiveté are gifts from the gods. Without them, we'd have known too much to start a business so personally demanding and professionally distracting from the work we wanted to do in the first place.

I think that our process is typical of the field of literary publishing (and all the other arts). A maturing publisher spends the first years completely absorbed in learning, via hard knocks, the meaning of the word "publish." Only when the varied basics of that discipline begin to be mastered can one turn to learning how to make and run an organization. Unfortunately, by the time the publisher is inclined to learn about how to manage a business effectively, there is in most cases a wild-child organization already there, leaving the publisher faced with some serious discipline problems. In the best world, a publisher of literature would be given the necessary tools, via handbooks, mentoring and technical assistance, to keep an ongoing balanced focus on art, organization and publishing. When Graywolf Press was founded, there were no such tools available, unless you were innocent enough (as we were) not to care if you seemed foolish asking questions of more-experienced publishers, all of whom were generous with their time.

We made the first Graywolf book, which took months of effort, and only then did it occur to us that we had to sell the copies we had made. Not thinking about marketing until we had a product is not what the business schools teach, I know, but I still don't think we were particularly stupid in delaying this realization. Publishing books requires the mastery of many crafts and areas of expertise—editing, design, bookmaking, marketing, cash management, accounting—and each area demands time and attention. There is little choice but to take them on one at a time.

We figured out—invented—marketing, and in doing so learned (by screwing up first) about invoices, discount schedules, the rules of consignment and the agonies of returns, how to sweet-talk bookstore folks and find free shipping materials, and the rudiments of time-management. (Rule #1: Do nothing but work.) We learned that it is best to keep a copy of the invoice because booksellers often lose theirs and call to ask you to send another copy.

But while we were enmeshed in our freshman year of the do-it-yourself-U's book marketing program, we were also starting to print our next book, and so simultaneously beginning our sophomore year studies of book editing and production. Soon we would begin our next phase of education—finance and accounting—and thus be engaged simultaneously in three courses of study, each of which is a completely absorbing career in itself. It occurs to me now that it is perhaps predictable that presses will do better at book editing and production than they will at learning finance, because their education starts out focused in one area and by the time the finance/management courses come up, the publisher is already engaged in several other fields of study.

I will admit here—with wavering hope that IRS agents are too knowledgeable about business to be thinking about starting a literary publishing company and therefore unlikely to read this manual (and some confidence that the statute of limitations is in effect)—that Graywolf Press failed to submit annual income tax forms for its first years. This failure greatly diminished our need for bookkeeping; but by dumb luck (and despite the *de rigeur* informality of that era) we did manage to invent and use bookkeeping anyway, mostly as a byproduct of applying common sense to the way we ran our business.

We used an Economix check register (a checkbook that allows you to keep track of expenses by category), and learned a few tricks along the way. We learned to use the float—perhaps one of the most mourned casualties along the information highway, as all companies start transferring funds electronically. We learned because of our eternally cash-poor situation to avoid "big" bills (anything over $100 was huge) by saving a percentage of every check that came in: a percentage went to a royalty account, a percentage to a reprint fund, etc. We learned, by way of some agonizing phone calls, that the printer's accounts-receivable person can actually be a friend by allowing us to set up a payment schedule on past-due bills. And from the accounts-receivable person, we learned that the squeaky A/R person gets paid and applied the principle to our own accounts. We realized we could serve our authors and audience only if we stayed in business, and so became willing to do whatever it took to achieve that end.

When we finally were forced by conscience (i.e., fear of getting caught) and grant requirements to file tax returns, we very sheepishly and apologetically lugged our bookkeeping system to a local accountant. Rather than scolding us for our haphazard hippie system, he congratulated us for inventing bookkeeping, all on our own. Simply by attending to the needs of our business and regularly balancing the checkbook, our economic house was, for the purpose of filing a tax return, in order.

A bit later on we had our first lesson in inventory management. During a year when our take-home pay was less than $6,000, we were told that we also had to pay taxes on the $8,000 worth of new books we had stored in our basement. It seemed that the IRS regarded unsold books as income. It took us two years to pay off the tax bill, and we never did sell half the copies of those books.

At that moment of realization, things suddenly became more complicated. That was when the simple tricks of the past stopped working, and when a cash guy woke up in an accrual world.

Professionalization

In hindsight, it seems to me that the key to the survival, or at least the vitality, of a small publishing company is finding the proper balance between professional demands and the entrepreneurial and amateur spirit that launched the venture. When finally you come face to face with the "wild child" organization that developed "by itself," without guidance, without the sort of careful shaping and ongoing education that characterized the development of your sense of book design, the tendency is either to run from it or hide it. By then, however, there are too many other people involved (employees, board members, funders) to let you do that.

When the fog clears, we have an entrepreneurial person who loves books, language and writing, still fully engaged (swamped, drowned) in lower- and higher-level education in literature, book design and production, book sales and promotion, fund-raising and board development, faced with the task of professionally managing an organization that is more than likely somewhat out of whack. Only the most successful publishers make it this far. It is daunting and discouraging to know that despite all your many successes there is yet another complex task to learn, and that in fact, your ability to come to terms with these alien, nonliterary skills will determine more than anything else whether you are ultimately successful.

There is a scientific field called "complexity" and I'm sure that many of its principles could be applied to literary and other nonprofit book publishing. From about the time an organization incorporates, things get enormously and increasingly complex. The very act of incorporation gives the organization a life of its own. This separate life coexists for a time with the organization's previous existence as someone's idea or pet project, then struggles for and achieves dominance.

Our business is affected by an increasing number of internal and external agents. Industry changes (just-in-time-inventory) begin to affect the way we manage our business. Managing cash and the problems of cash flow become more difficult as an organization grows, to the point that it could be the central issue of running a small publishing company. Finance under an accrual accounting system requires very different forms of analysis and understanding than the I-know-what-I-can-see cash system. There are no rules and guides—or rather there are many rules and many guides, no three of which agree. None of us define "cost of books sold" in the same way. We learn that if one has employees, one has to manage them. (Every employee added, even if you've got a staff of eight, seems to double the time it takes to manage—in other words, the number of times we are interrupted during the day, which is how most of us think of management.) We need to learn how to hire people in areas in which we have little personal expertise.[1]

Faced with quickly changing industry conditions, uncertainty of the economy and the needs of people who depend on you and your business, financial and organizational needs begin to battle against mission. Title lists need balance of income potential, as well as of literary style. We are determined to keep books in print, but finance committee members more frequently mention the amount of money we have tied up in "inventory." (It isn't "inventory" we say to ourselves, it represents individual copies of an author's heart and soul. But, we know, we really know, it is also inventory—in other words, dollars we can't use.) Shall we keep the retail price as is and scare off our audience?

These and other organizational and financial issues force themselves upon us at a time when we are already completely overwhelmed with the work of helping literature find an audience. The issues sneak up on us, a bit at a time, problem by problem, crisis by crisis, near-disaster. Suddenly it seems all we have time to think of are organizational and financial issues; we are so tangled in their thickets that we can barely see the trees, much less the forest.

Whether yours is organized as a for-profit or nonprofit entity, making an organization work—from board development through staffing, from the budget through the audit—is the last piece of the puzzle for making a book-publishing operation work. It is the most difficult part, and if you don't come to terms with it, you certainly won't reach your potential as a publisher, you won't be satisfied as a worker and the organization may not survive.

We need to be prescient enough to take time to rethink and reinvent our organizations, with a clear-eyed understanding of our artistic mission and lack of knee-jerk attachment to the ways things have always been done. You need to be sure that your governance is best suited to the organization you are and will be, that your accounting, auditing and financial activities give you information you can understand and use to run your business better, that you and your funders understand the financial requirements of the publishing business (half a grant is worse than none) and that your way of doing business and your mission keep up with the rapidly changing marketplace.

[1]Hiring people goes through three phases of complexity and sophistication: because we are offering low pay, we can first only hire a body; when we learn more and pay more, we can hire a mind; and if we learn even more, we can hire the right mind—and fail, and try again.

What we have needed is a guide through these issues, one that would enable us to tackle them head-on, a set of reasonable options we can choose from, the voice of someone who has taken the time to think through issues we ordinarily have to deal with on the fly. Now we have one! Thank heaven! With this guidebook and an inclination to share information with our peers, we may be able to turn our attention back to the core things that brought us into this business in the first place. We might even have time to read a book! The financial and operational issues won't go away, but we will have a framework for dealing with them.

....

Biographical Note

Scott Walker was, in his words, "chief bottle-washer" at Graywolf Press from 1974 to 1994. Since then, he has been a writer, consultant in publishing and planning, free-lance editor and publisher of books and electronic journalism.

foreword

The Nonprofit Press

The publishing field has experienced many changes over the past hundred years. Until the 19th century, American book publishing was a simple cottage industry with no distinction between seller and printer. The cost of printing a book was paid by the author's patron, sometimes by the individual author. With the rise of a mass market for books, however, these relationships began to change. Today, the publishing scene is dominated by large commercial houses with significant promotion and distribution power, large scales of operation and substantial levels of capital available to them. The largest trade publisher has access to $2 billion in capital. A small nonprofit, on the other hand, may only have access to a few thousand dollars.

Despite differences in scale and market share, publishers of all types—large commercial houses, university presses, independent presses and nonprofit presses—face similar issues of acquiring manuscripts, editing and producing books, and marketing and distributing them. So what distinguishes these publishers from each other? For nonprofit literary presses, the answer lies in their mission. Nonprofit literary presses developed to fill a gap in the market through the publication of serious creative literature.

Serious creative literature has almost never been able to sustain itself financially in the marketplace. Traditionally, it has found support in one of three sources: wealthy individual patrons, universities to the extent that they publish literary titles, and commercial publishing houses that cover losses on literary titles with profits earned on books that succeed in the mass market. These sources of support for literary publishing have become less substantial, as well as less dependable, over the past few decades. Within this context, nonprofit literary presses have created a unique niche for themselves that is defined by the types of books they publish.

Nonprofit literary presses are diverse. Some work to restore and preserve important works that have gone out of print; others promote work by younger and less well-known authors; while others focus on translation, experimental fiction and poetry. At least 50 such nonprofit presses are on file with the Council of Literary Magazines and Presses (New York); many other independent presses are exploring the possibility of becoming nonprofits.

It is for you, the nonprofit press, that this resource manual is written. We know from our work with the Mellon Foundation's nonprofit press program that nonprofit financial management is generally more complex and demanding than a for-profit business of similar size. While similar in many respects to other publishers, the nonprofit press industry is unique both in terms of its organizational demands and its sources of capitalization. Not only must a nonprofit press account for all of the financial transactions that occur as a result of the production and selling of its books, it must also account for contributed income and fulfill the various reporting requirements of each of its funders.

This manual is designed to walk you through the financial management issues of a nonprofit press. The first bit of advice we would give you is this: Relax! Take this handbook a chapter at a time. Study the examples. Refer to the glossary and index. And above all else, remember that the ultimate goal is for your press to achieve its mission in the most effective way possible. Financial management is simply a tool to help you reach that end.

chapter 1

On Being Nonprofit

Chapter Highlights

▶ **Taking the First Steps**

▶ **Applying for Tax-Exemption**

▶ **Tying Up the Loose Ends**

▶ **Establishing Your Board of Directors**

▶ **Governance Responsibilities of the Board**

▶ **The Role of the Treasurer and Finance Committee**

On Being Nonprofit

Nonprofit organizations vary greatly in size, mission and scope. They include local churches and synagogues, large hospitals, human service agencies, professional associations, arts organizations, sports leagues, museums, colleges and foundations. Some nonprofits operate on shoe-string budgets with no full-time paid staff, while others look remarkably like large corporations with million-dollar budgets and sophisticated operating systems.

So what makes a nonprofit different from a for-profit business? The primary distinction lies in the fact that in a nonprofit, any surplus of income over expenses—otherwise known as profit—must be used to further fulfill the organization's mission. In private companies and publicly held corporations, owners or shareholders benefit from the firms' profits. In a nonprofit, no one owns the right to share in the organization's profits or surpluses; it all goes back to the organization itself.

The very term "nonprofit" is somewhat misleading. Such a designation does not mean the organization either should not or cannot earn a profit. On the contrary, a surplus of income over expenses is essential if an organization is to be financially viable. "Nonprofit" refers to the fundamental distinction that an organization exists for a goal other than earning a profit for its owners. In recent years, many of these types of organizations have begun to refer to themselves as "not-for-profits" to better clarify that their tax-exempt status stems from their central missions, not from their ability or inability to be profitable.

In the United States, tax laws define nonprofits as groups organized for charitable or mutual-benefit purposes. More than 1 million organizations, representing the majority of nonprofits in the country, have achieved tax-exempt status under the Internal Revenue Code (IRC). In addition to being exempt from paying income taxes, many nonprofits are also exempted from sales and real estate taxation, depending on local regulations. Gifts to many, though not all, nonprofits are also tax deductible for donors, providing an added benefit for both the organization and its contributors.

A Rose by Any Other Name...

Many terms are applied to the nonprofit sector, often interchangeably: voluntary, independent, third sector, charitable and tax-exempt. Each of these terms gives a partial understanding of the sector, yet they are equally limiting. For instance, while volunteers are often integral to the governance and staffing of nonprofits, most of the sector's activity is carried out by paid employees. The term "charitable" recognizes the public charitable intent of many nonprofits, as well as the support that they receive from donations and grants. Yet not all nonprofits are incorporated as charitable, and contributed support does not constitute the only, or even the major, source of most nonprofits' revenues.

In fact, the very term nonprofit can be somewhat misleading. "Nonprofit" refers to the fundamental distinction that an organization exists for a goal other than earning a profit for its owners; profits (excess revenue) that are generated in a given year must be diverted back into the organization. The term nonprofit does not mean that the organization either should not or cannot make a profit. On the contrary, a surplus is essential for the functioning of a financially viable organization. Likewise, a private business cannot designate itself as a "nonprofit" just because it is operating in the red, even though it may seem like an apt description!

The IRS categorizes nonprofits into 27 groups. In most cases, however, the term "nonprofit" refers to those organizations incorporated under the section 501(c)(3) classification. This is the classification under which most literary nonprofit presses fall. In addition to providing tax exemption, a 501(c)(3) classification is important for your press because foundations, in general, are unable to make grants to organizations that do not have this particular designation. Other organizations that may qualify for a 501(c)(3) status under the Internal Revenue Code include those whose primary purpose (their "exempt purpose") is:

- religious;
- educational;
- charitable;
- scientific;
- literary;
- related to testing for public safety;
- fostering national or international amateur sports competition; or
- for the prevention of cruelty to children or animals.

Taking the First Steps

Though somewhat tedious, the process for incorporating as a nonprofit is relatively simple. The first steps are to determine your organization's purpose and structure and to form an initial board of directors (most states require at least three members). Contact the secretary of state's office for specific forms, costs and detailed instructions for incorporation in your particular state. Because incorporation is a legal issue that varies from state to state, we strongly recommend that you consult with an attorney familiar with nonprofit law at the start of the process, if not throughout it.

Once you have a board of directors in place, you can begin creating the documents you will need to apply for both recognition as a nonprofit corporation in your state and for federal and state tax-exempt status. Among these initial documents, most state nonprofit corporation laws require that organizations file *articles of incorporation* and *bylaws*. Articles of incorporation typically contain a statement of the organization's purposes and its legal powers and authority, including limitations on powers and authority. It may also contain governance provisions, such as how board members will be selected. In order for your organization to eventually qualify for tax-exempt status, the articles of incorporation must also specify that, upon dissolution of the organization, any remaining assets will be distributed for a public or charitable purpose. Bylaws make up the "rule book" for running the organization.

Once your application is approved, the state will send you a *charter* or *certificate of incorporation*, giving your organization the right to do business in your state. Early on, you should establish a record keeping system to preserve these corporate documents, the minutes of all board meetings and any legal notices, such as notification of tax exemption. These official records must be maintained for the life of your small press.

Applying for Tax Exemption

After your press is incorporated as a nonprofit organization, you may apply for exemption from federal corporate income taxes. The forms and documentation you will need include the following:

- **IRS Form 1023**, *"Application for Recognition of Exemption Under Section 501(c)(3) of the IRC."*
- A **conformed copy** of your press's:
  - certificate of incorporation;
  - articles of incorporation; and
  - bylaws.

  A conformed copy is one that agrees with the original, including all amendments, and is signed by a principal officer of the organization.
- Financial data, as requested.
- Documentation showing that your organization has a board of directors with at least three members, including a president.

Again, even if you prepare the application yourself, it is a good idea to have an attorney review your application before sending it in.

In addition to completing the proper applications, forms and documents discussed above, organizations applying for exemption are required to complete two other steps:

- **Pay a User Fee**—The law requires the payment of a user fee for determination-letter requests. IRS Form 8718 *"User Fee for Exempt Organizations Determination Request"* should be used to determine the amount of fee that must be paid. The payment must accompany the application request. The IRS will not process the request unless the fee has been paid.

- **Employer Identification Number**—Every exempt organization is required to have an employer identification number (EIN), whether or not it has any employees. If your organization does not have an EIN, it should complete IRS Form SS-4 *"Application for Employer Identification Number."* Once the EIN is received, your organization must also apply for a state employer identification number.

The IRS applies two tests when considering eligibility for tax-exempt status: the "organizational test" and the "operational test." The *organizational test* looks at the purposes around which your press is organized. The IRS will review your articles of incorporation (or other creating documents) to ensure that your press is limited to one or more exempt purposes and that its assets will be distributed for a public or charitable purpose upon dissolution of the press. Your press must meet the requirements of the *operational test* on an ongoing basis through its actual activities. To pass this test, your press must engage primarily in activities that accomplish one or more of the exempt purposes outlined in its articles of incorporation.

The IRS will notify you in writing if your press satisfies the requirements for tax exemption under section 501(c)(3). This notice will also tell you if contributions your press may receive are tax-deductible for private donors. Along with the notification, you will be informed of requirements for filing an annual information return, usually Form 990, *"Return of Organization Exempt from Income Tax."* (See Chapter 6 for more information on tax and compliance reporting requirements.)

Tying Up the Loose Ends

The forms and filings don't end with the receipt of your notice of federal tax exemption. In most states, a separate application is required for exemption from *state income tax*, after your 501(c)(3) status has been established.

Your nonprofit may be exempt from paying corporate income tax, but it is not exempt from taxes on employees' wages, such as Social Security taxes under FICA, employee income tax withholdings or state and federal unemployment insurance taxes. In fact, if social security taxes and withholdings are not paid in full and on time, board members and administrators may be held personally liable for taxes and penalties of up to 100 percent of all taxes due.

Depending on state and local regulations, you may also need to:

*   file a *charitable trust registration* with the state;
*   apply for a solicitation license from the local municipality;
*   comply with state worker's compensation requirements;
*   register with the state unemployment insurance program;
*   apply for property tax exemption with the local tax assessor's office;
*   obtain liability insurance; and
*   apply for a nonprofit bulk mail permit from the post office.

Be aware also that, depending on your press's type of program and sources of funding, further registration, reporting or licensing may be required.

Establishing Your Board of Directors

Nonprofit organizations are required to have boards of directors. The board of directors is legally responsible for your press's well-being. Its duties include overseeing the overall financial health of the press and ensuring that the press is fulfilling its mission as stated in the press's charter or articles of incorporation. The board is the entity to which the press's senior administrative staff report.

Board members have a *fiduciary* obligation to act in good faith and in the best interests of the organization they serve. This means they have been entrusted with the well-being of the organization, especially its financial health. Board members are expected to exercise sound business judgment and reasonable care when making decisions for the organization. Individual board members must take special care to ensure that their decisions are not influenced by interests outside of the organization. In some cases, it's appropriate for a board member to refrain from voting on a specific matter, if he or she has a personal conflict of interest. The board's duty is to remain faithful to the organization's mission and to make decisions that are consistent with the organization's central goals.

The following are examples of the many activities members can expect to be involved in during their service on the board:

*   setting organizational policy;
*   making sure the press has the financial and human resources necessary to achieve its mission;
*   supervising executive management; and
*   guiding long-range planning.

The board of directors of any organization needs to stay well-informed about the programmatic and financial activity of the organization, while also keeping a pulse on the larger community. Balancing these demands is not easy; board members walk a delicate line between becoming too involved in the details of internal, day-to-day issues and not being informed enough about operational issues to make wise decisions for the organization.

Judicious selection of board members is important. Each board member will bring his or her own expertise and talents to help your press achieve its goals. A nonprofit press should recruit board members to reflect a diversity of:

- publishing experience;
- fund-raising ability;
- connections with the broader community (for example, literary connections or special interest connections, depending on the purpose of your press);
- financial and business management knowledge; and
- gender, age and other characteristics.

Generally speaking, most nonprofit boards range in size from 10 to 20 members. Legally, however, you may need as few as three.

Governance Responsibilities of the Board

1. Establish and maintain the organization within all legal and governmental guidelines.

2. Organize the board for maximum effectiveness.

3. Establish the organization's mission and long-term objectives.

4. Establish performance standards for board members.

5. Identify talents and skills necessary to maintain an effective board.

6. Replenish the board with needed talents and skills as openings appear.

7. Establish performance goals and standards for senior administrative staff.

8. Hire senior administrative staff.

9. Establish and monitor fiscal controls.

10. Monitor senior staff performance.

11. Develop funding adequate to the organization's program and fiscal needs.

12. Establish and maintain a public relations program.

13. Monitor the impact of the organization on the community.

Expectations of board membership should be clearly defined. Written policies should include:

- attendance requirements;
- committee structure and membership;
- legal liabilities for board members;
- expectations for fund-raising;
- length of terms for members; and
- nomination procedures.

Finally, the board's work should be delegated through a committee structure. Most nonprofit boards include a personnel committee, a nominating committee and a finance and development committee.

....

The Role of the Treasurer and Finance Committee

We cannot overstate the importance of the board's treasurer and finance committee. It is their role to stay on top of financial matters and present this information to the rest of the board in a meaningful and timely fashion. If you, as a board member, are not financially astute, you need to make sure there are other board members who have this particular expertise. The bottom line is that *every member of the board is responsible for the continuation of the nonprofit and liable for any mistakes made by the organization.*

The treasurer and finance committee are primarily concerned with two aspects of the nonprofit's financial resources:

- ensuring that the organization has secured enough revenue or financing for current and future needs; and
- overseeing the press's financial position to meet legal requirements.

More specifically, the committee oversees fund-raising, approves the annual budget, arranges for audits and reviews and presents monthly financial reports to the board.

The treasurer and other finance committee members should help translate the press's financial data into useful information the entire board can use in making sound policy decisions. Reports should clearly indicate if the press is on target with planned expenses and revenue, if it is financially solvent (enough money in the bank to pay current expenses) and if it has enough income to meet future expenses. The treasurer and finance committee's reports should enable all board members to accurately answer the questions in the box on the next page. You'll find further discussion of the board's specific roles in the press's financial functions in Chapters 2 and 4.

Can You Answer These Questions?

The following questions are posed by William Bowen, president of The Andrew W. Mellon Foundation, in his book, **Inside the Boardroom: Governance by Directors and Trustees** (John Wiley & Sons, New York, 1995). He suggests that every board member should be able to answer them. How well do you do?

- Is the organization in approximate financial equilibrium?

- Does the organization have sufficient liquidity (cash flow) and flexible funds to withstand temporary adversity?

- Is the organization's capital base being eroded to pay operating expenses or to handle deferred maintenance? Is the capital base growing fast enough to meet future needs?

- What is the organization's fund-raising record? How do its fund-raising results compare with those of similar organizations?

- How vulnerable are the finances of the organization to changes in the circumstances or priorities of key donors? How diverse are its funders?

- How much debt is outstanding, and is it clear how the debt is to be serviced?

chapter 2
....

Preparing
the Annual Budget

Chapter Highlights

▶ **Budgeting for Book Income and Expenses**

▶ **Preparing a Fund-Raising Budget**

▶ **Bringing It All Together: The Master Budget**

▶ **Budget Approval**

▶ **The Budget as a Financial Tool**

Preparing the Annual Budget

Effective budgeting is a prerequisite for the successful financial management of any press. Two or three months before the beginning of each fiscal year, the board of directors and management of your press should meet to discuss and decide on specific goals and objectives for the upcoming year. Once these decisions are made, the next step is to prepare an annual budget. A budget is a "plan of action" for future activities. Budgeting is the process of converting your press's strategic goals and objectives into dollars and cents.

To be effective, the budgeting process should be a team effort using the skills and knowledge of people at all levels of the organization. The individuals involved in budgeting and the roles they play will generally depend on the size and structure of your press. Usually, management or staff are responsible for developing preliminary revenue and expense projections and for making budget recommendations to the board; however, it is ultimately the board of directors' responsibility to approve the final budget.

The board is legally responsible for ensuring that the budget is:

- fiscally sound;
- developed to further the press's tax-exempt purpose; and
- in compliance with applicable laws and regulations.

Some of the policies the board should establish in the budget process include requirements for a balanced budget, policies on the use of cash reserves and decisions about salary increases, hiring, layoffs, new programs, capital projects and major fund-raising efforts.

In addition to reviewing and approving the budget, the board is also responsible for monitoring the actual financial activity during the year, comparing this information to the budget and approving any plans for corrective action if the need arises.

Management, too, has specific responsibilities and duties in the budget-development process. These include:

*   communicating budgeting policies and procedures to other managers and program staff;
*   establishing the format for budget requests;
*   developing revenue and expenditure forecasts;
*   reviewing budget requests and making resource allocation decisions;
*   presenting the proposed budget to the board, explaining its provisions and possible consequences and answering board member questions.

Using the list of goals and objectives for the upcoming year as a guide, the starting point in the budget development process should be to assemble prior years' budgets and actual financial statements. Using this information as a reference, detailed revenue and expense projections for the upcoming year should then be prepared. This is easier said than done as there are several steps to this part of the budgeting process that must be addressed before a final proposed budget for the whole press can be completed.

We strongly recommend that your press use a process called *income-based budgeting* when compiling the projections for the budget. The premise behind income-based budgeting is that you first project all of the future income the press knows of and can reasonably expect to receive and then budget your expenses based on this projected income. This minimizes the possibility that the press will budget expenses for which no identifiable source of income is available.

Budgeting for Book Income and Expenses

A logical place to start the budget process is to prepare detailed income and expense projections for the books identified in your plan to be published in the coming year. Use a form similar to Figure 2-1 (page 14) to project the budget for each book on your upcoming list.

Book sales may well be the most difficult item to project. Few people, if any, have perfected the process of budgeting for book sales in the small nonprofit publishing field. Because you are coming out with a new frontlist each year, it's tough to know which books will sell well and which ones won't. Factoring in backlist sales is just as difficult—and then to complicate things further, you will also need to establish a budget for sales returns. To arrive at a budget for book sales, your best bet is to rely on past experience and your knowledge of the current economic climate in the publishing industry. Also, be conservative in your projections. Overly optimistic sales projections may look good on paper, but if they don't materialize the consequences for your press may be dire.

Figure 2-1

Projecting Income
and Expenses
Per Book

Individual Book Budget

Specific Book Information

Title	*Where the Wind Blows*
Trim Size	6" x 9"
Number of Pages	250
Photos	0
Cover	4-Color
Binding	Paper
Sales Price	$12.95
Royalty Rate	7.50%
Royalty Rate Base	Retail
First Printing	4,000
Publication Date	December 1996

Financial Information

Account Description	Budget Amount
EARNED INCOME	
Direct Sales	$ 2,500
Distributor Sales	48,000
Wholesale Sales	- 0 -
(Discounts)	(20,000)
(Returns)	(10,100)
(Returns Processing Fee)	(400)
(Refunds)	- 0 -
Subsidiary Rights Sales	- 0 -
Projected Total Earned Income	**20,000**
COST OF BOOKS SOLD	
1) Inventoriable Costs:	
Acquisition/Agent Fees	- 0 -
Permission Fees	- 0 -
Rights Payments	- 0 -
Translation Fees	- 0 -
Cover Design/Artwork	1,000
Copyediting	500
Proofreading	300
Typesetting	1,500
Paper, Printing & Binding	4,400
Shipping (Manufacturing)	600
Total Inventoriable Costs	**8,300**
2) Non-Inventoriable Costs:	
Royalty Expense	3,900
Distribution Fees	6,100
Total Non-Inventoriable Costs	**10,000**
Projected Total Cost of Books Sold	**18,300**
Net Projected Gross Profit	**$ 1,700**

In preparing expense projections for each book, include all costs that are directly related to producing the book in-house plus distribution fees and royalties. For budgeting purposes, salary expenses are not included here, though the cost of services by outside consultants, such as designers, editors or proofreaders, would be.

Once an income and expense projection has been prepared for each book, each of these individual book budgets should be combined into a spreadsheet to arrive at a total book income and expense budget for the coming year. An example of how this spreadsheet might be formatted appears in the worksheet appendix on page 109. The total amounts computed on this spreadsheet will now become a part of the total budget.

Preparing a Fund-Raising Budget

As a nonprofit press, income from book sales represents only a portion of the total income required to run the press. The remaining income (usually anywhere from 40 percent to 60 percent of total income) comes from foundation and corporate grants, individual contributions, board support, special fund-raising events, government grants or contracts, interest income and the like. Because of your press's dependence on these other sources of income, preparing an accurate budget becomes extremely important.

Use a three-tiered approach for preparing your fund-raising budget. To do this, identify income sources using the following categories:

- income you know is *confirmed* or that you are *highly* confident of receiving;
- income you expect or feel reasonably certain of receiving; and
- income that has a possibility of being received, but is currently very uncertain.

The total of all three columns represents the *best-case-scenario* projected income for the year. For the income-based budget your press ultimately adopts, however, the income amount should only reflect the confirmed amounts and possibly the reasonably certain amounts. *Do not* include the uncertain amounts; and don't try to balance the budget by including an item entitled "income to be raised." If the uncertain income materializes or if you raise additional funds beyond those already confirmed, that's great. You now have the opportunity to adjust your expense budget accordingly. But if the uncertain funds do not materialize, you are still in a fairly safe position because you were not relying on those amounts to cover budgeted expenses.

When projecting *fund-raising income,* we recommend using a form similar to the one presented in Figure 2-2 (page 16). Please note that given today's uncertain fund-raising climate, budgeting for contributions may be difficult. If you want a balanced budget, *__be conservative__*.

Figure 2-2

Projecting Your
Fund-Raising
Budget

Fund-Raising Budget

Income Sources	Last Year's Actual	Current Year Budget	Proposed Budget—Next Year		
			Confirmed	Reasonably Certain	Uncertain
Foundation Grants:					
1)	_____	_____	_____	_____	_____
2)	_____	_____	_____	_____	_____
3)	_____	_____	_____	_____	_____
4)	_____	_____	_____	_____	_____
5)	_____	_____	_____	_____	_____
Total Foundation Grants	_____	_____	_____	_____	_____
Corporate Grants:					
1)	_____	_____	_____	_____	_____
2)	_____	_____	_____	_____	_____
3)	_____	_____	_____	_____	_____
Total Corporate Grants	_____	_____	_____	_____	_____
Government Grants:					
1)	_____	_____	_____	_____	_____
2)	_____	_____	_____	_____	_____
3)	_____	_____	_____	_____	_____
Total Government Grants	_____	_____	_____	_____	_____
Other Sources:					
Individual Contributions	_____	_____	_____	_____	_____
Board Support	_____	_____	_____	_____	_____
Sponsorships	_____	_____	_____	_____	_____
In-Kind Contributions	_____	_____	_____	_____	_____
Special Events Income	_____	_____	_____	_____	_____
Interest Income	_____	_____	_____	_____	_____
Other Income	_____	_____	_____	_____	_____
Total of Other Sources	_____	_____	_____	_____	_____
Fund-Raising Income— All Sources	_____	_____	_____	_____	_____

Bringing It All Together: The Master Budget

Once you've completed your book and fund-raising budgets, you're ready to transfer these numbers to a master budget. Figure 2-3 (page 18) presents a master-budget format that allows you to clearly see how much fund-raising support your press requires to break even for the year. Note, too, that we've included a "Prior Year Actual" column. This is your reality check to help ensure that the income and expenses you've projected have some relevance to past experience. All that's left now is to project operations expenses. For the most part these expenses will mirror the previous year's expenses, unless there have been significant changes in costs from one year to the next.

Budget Approval

The final budget proposal should be submitted to the board of directors for ratification. Assuming all budget assumptions have been properly documented and detailed budget worksheets have been prepared, the board may only need to see a summary for approval and not the detailed worksheets. As noted earlier, the budgeting process will probably involve many people and it is important that you use all available resources to develop a reliable budget. Ultimately, however, it is the board of directors' responsibility to approve this budget, thereby endorsing and committing themselves to the resulting plan of action.

The Budget as a Financial Tool

In addition to expressing your press's plan of action in monetary terms, the budget also functions as a financial tool that should be used as a benchmark for assessing actual financial activity throughout the year. If used appropriately, this tool can provide management an early warning sign in the event that the press's financial goals are not being met. The key here is to incorporate your budget into the ongoing accounting process. Don't assume that just preparing and approving the budget is enough. Use the budget to compare against actual financial activity on a month-to-date and year-to-date basis and investigate any variances between the actual and budgeted amounts as they arise. This information can help you know if the press is heading in the right direction according to its plan or if it has swerved off course. If the latter is the case, investigate the cause and look for ways to get it back on course.

Summary

A well-founded and carefully prepared budget is crucial to the successful and effective financial management of your press. It provides the financial and operational guidance necessary to implement board policies and directives and it provides management with the tools to measure the press's immediate and long-term financial health.

Preparation of the annual budget involves many individuals and several interrelated procedures, culminating in a final approved budget for the whole press. Once approved, the budget must be compared to actual results on a timely basis throughout the year to ensure the press is operating according to plan and if not, that corrective action is taken by the board or management to put it back on track.

Figure 2-3
Total
Press Budget

Total Press Budget

For Fiscal Year _____ to _____

	Prior Year Actual	Current Year Budget	Projected Current Year Actual	Proposed Budget Next Year
Book Income				
Direct Sales	$	$	$	$
Distributor Sales				
Wholesale Sales				
(Discounts)				
(Sales Returns)				
(Returns Processing Fees)				
(Refunds)				
Net Sales				
Subsidiary Rights Income				
Total Book Income				
Cost of Books Sold				
Inventory Beginning of Year				
Acquisition/Agent Fees				
Permission Fees				
Rights Payments				
Translation Fees				
Cover Design/Artwork				
Copyediting				
Proofreading				
Typesetting				
Paper, Printing & Binding				
Shipping				
Obsolete Inventory Adjustment				
Cost of Books Available for Sale				
Less: Inventory End of Year				
Total Production Costs				
Royalty Expense				
Distribution Fees				
Total Cost of Books Sold				
Gross Profit	$	$	$	$

(continued)

Figure 2-3
Total
Press Budget
(continued)

Total Press Budget

For Fiscal Year _____ to _____

	Prior Year Actual	Current Year Budget	Projected Current Year Actual	Proposed Budget Next Year
Operating Expenses				
Salaries	$	$	$	$
Payroll Taxes				
Employee Benefits				
Professional Fees				
Outside Editorial Services				
Supplies				
Telephone				
Postage and Shipping				
Occupancy				
Equip. Rental and Maint.				
Insurance				
Travel				
Trade Show Expense				
Advertising and Promotions				
Catalog Expense				
Review Copies				
Other Fund-Raising Expense				
Employee Training				
Conferences and Conventions				
Interest Expense				
Dues and Subscriptions				
Bank Charges				
Miscellaneous				
Amortization				
Depreciation				
Total Operating Expenses				
Deficit from Operations				
Support & Other Income				
Foundation Grants				
Corporate Grants				
Government Grants				
Individual Contributions				
Board Support				
Sponsorships				
In-Kind Contributions				
Special Events Income				
(Special Event Expenses)				
Interest/Investment Income				
Other Income				
Total Support & Other Income				
Surplus (Deficit)	$	$	$	$

chapter 3

Keeping the Books

Chapter Highlights

▶ **Cash Basis vs. Accrual Basis Accounting**

▶ **The Double-Entry System**

▶ **Chart of Accounts**

▶ **Registers, Journals and Ledgers**

Keeping the Books

A s much as your press needs a budget for projecting anticipated sources and uses of funds, it will also need a system for tracking actual income and expenses as they occur. The tracking system that organizes your press's financial activity is called *bookkeeping* or *accounting*. Accounting information, if properly presented and understood, allows you to make informed decisions that let you evaluate, in monetary terms, the effectiveness of your press.

Like it or not, you need accounting to run a business. And even though your press has elected a nonprofit status, it is still a business. Computer accounting software has made it easier for many small businesses of all kinds to maintain accurate and up-to-date financial records, without the expense of a full-time bookkeeper or an outside accountant. But like its predecessor printed accounting forms, accounting software is only as good as the knowledge of the person using it.

You don't need an accounting degree to manage your press's finances. But even with a good accounting software package, you still need a basic understanding of accounting terms, of how information flows through the accounting system and what useful information the system can provide. A basic knowledge of the accounting procedures will also enable you to select a software package that best meets your press's needs. Reading this chapter won't make you an accountant, but it will give you a working knowledge of the basic accounting principles and procedures you will need to successfully manage and account for the resources of your small press, with or without a computer.

Cash Basis vs. Accrual Basis Accounting

Many small businesses and nonprofits make the mistake of trying to account for their financial transactions on a *cash basis*. Accounting on the cash basis means that income is recorded only when cash is received and expenses are not recorded until they have actually been paid. Although the cash basis of accounting is the simplest way to keep financial records, it is only appropriate for individuals or for private-practice professionals, such as attorneys or other consultants, who are selling a service with little or no inventory of goods and few, if any, employees. The cash basis of accounting is not appropriate for a small press because it does not take into account book inventories, amounts of money the press owes to others (accounts payable) or amounts others owe the press (accounts receivable).

The alternative to cash basis accounting is the *accrual basis of accounting*. Of the two approaches, the accrual basis is really the only one that can present the true financial condition of your press because it records *all* income and expenses, whether paid or not. Under the accrual method, income is recorded when it is earned and expenses are recorded when they are incurred, regardless of whether any cash has been received or paid. Your press must use the accrual method if it is to accurately account for book inventories, authors' royalties, payroll expenses (especially withholdings and taxes), grants designated for particular purposes and a host of other specifics.

The other reason for choosing the accrual over the cash basis of accounting is that, at some time, your press may be required to have its financial statements audited by a certified public accountant (CPA). If your press is to pass such an audit, its financial records must be prepared in conformance with generally accepted accounting principles (GAAP)—and that means accounting on the accrual basis.

....

The Double-Entry System

The *double-entry system* is based on the premise that every financial transaction has two sides. By recording both sides of a transaction using the double-entry system, you ensure that your financial assets do not disappear into thin air unnoticed.

The financial statements of your press (see Chapter 4) have several major categories: assets, liabilities, net assets, book sales, cost of books sold, operating expenses, contributions and other income.

Within these major categories are numerous subcategories called *accounts*. The entire group of accounts is called the *general ledger*. Every financial transaction your press records affects at least *two* accounts and each account has two sides to keep track of resources coming in and going out. The left-hand side of accounts in the ledger is the *debit* side; the right-hand side is called the *credit* side (Figure 3-1). Debits are also sometimes called *charges*. For every transaction, at least one account is always debited, or "charged," (meaning an entry is made to the left side) and at least one account is always credited (an entry is made to the right side). The rule is that debits must always equal credits.

Figure 3-1

Basic Format for
Account Ledgers

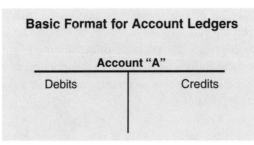

Basic Format for Account Ledgers

Account "A"

Debits	Credits

One of the advantages of the double-entry system is the ease of determining the current balance of each account and exactly how much money has gone into and out of each account in a given period. This is done simply by totaling each column and then subtracting the totals to get the current balance.

Looking specifically at the balance sheet, and without getting too technical, accounts listed under assets (cash, book inventory, accounts receivable and so on) normally have *debit balances*, meaning the total of the left side is greater than the total of the right side. Accounts listed under liabilities (accounts payable, loans, accrued salaries) normally have credit balances. A *credit balance,* in this case, simply means the total of the right side of an account is greater than the total of the left side.

Let's look at a simplified example to better illustrate the double-entry system. (Notice that the dollar amount of each transaction is followed by a small number; use this to help you see where each amount is posted in the accounts below.) Say your press prints a small run (1,000 copies) of its very first book and the printer charges you \$3,000[1] (\$3 per book). For the moment, assume that the book cost you nothing to produce but the printing fee—you wrote it yourself, edited it, did the typesetting and page layout entirely in-house. When you receive the books on March 1, you also receive a bill for the printing. You would record these transactions in the following way:

Example

Balance Sheet Accounts

Assets: Book Inventory		Liabilities: Accounts Payable	
Debits	Credits	Debits	Credits
3/1 \$3,000[1]			3/1 \$3,000[1]

Later in the month (March 15), your press receives a check for \$2,000[2] in fulfillment of a grant to cover part of the expenses for publishing the book, and you pay the printer \$2,000[3] the next day (March 16). (On January 1, you had received notice that the grant was approved, and you posted it to the account "Grants Receivable"). On March 20, you fill your first order for 100 copies at a price of \$10 each (total \$1,000[4]) and you bill the agency that placed the order. Cost of the books sold is \$300[5] (100 copies at \$3 per copy for printing). Your entries for these transactions would be as follows:

Balance Sheet Accounts

Assets:

Cash

Debits	Credits
3/15 $2,000[2]	3/16 $2,000[3]

(Account balance: $0)

Accounts Receivable

Debits	Credits
3/20 $1,000[4]	

(Account balance: $1,000 debit)

Grants Receivable

Debits	Credits
1/1 $2,000	3/15 $2,000[2]

(Account balance: $0)

Book Inventory

Debits	Credits
3/1 $3,000[1]	3/20 $300[5]

(Account balance: $2,700 debit)

Liabilities:

Accounts Payable

Debits	Credits
3/16 $2,000[3]	3/1 $3,000[1]

(Account balance: $1,000 credit)

Statement of Activities Accounts

Book Sales

Debits	Credits
	3/20 $1,000[4]

(Account balance: $1,000 credit)

Contributed Income

Debits	Credits
	1/1 $2,000

(Account balance: $2,000 credit)

Cost of Books Sold

Debits	Credits
3/20 $300[5]	

(Account balance: $300 debit)

It is important for you to understand how the double-entry system works, even if your accounting software seems to take care of making the appropriate debits and credits for you. Once you understand this system, it will be much easier for you to find errors if the accounts fail to balance.

Chart of Accounts

To facilitate the tracking of all of your press's financial transactions, you need to develop a comprehensive listing of the accounts you use and plan to use. This listing, called a *chart of accounts*, identifies each account with a name and a number.

How your press chooses to organize its chart of accounts will depend on a number of factors, including:

- the level of detail you wish to achieve;
- the type of accounting software you are using or plan to use;
- whether you plan to internally account for transactions by department, by net asset class or by book; and
- the skill level and understanding of the person performing most of the accounting functions.

There's no magic formula for developing a chart of accounts. The thing to keep in mind is that the chart of accounts forms the foundation for the flow of information through the accounting system and ultimately allows you to arrive at the final product—the financial statements.

The chart of accounts will always include more accounts than will appear on your financial statements. The accounts listed in the chart are actually subaccounts to the major accounts listed on the balance sheet and statement of activities, enabling you to track the details of where money goes, without complicating the final financial statements. Too much detail in a financial statement (especially one presented to the board of directors or outside readers) can cause confusion and detract the reader from understanding the overall financial picture. Figure 3-2 (page 27) and Figure 3-3 (page 28) provide detailed charts of accounts for balance sheet accounts and statement of activities accounts, respectively. Line items listed in the chart of accounts without an account number represent subtotals and totals computed on the actual financial statements.

Much thought should be given to the initial set-up of the chart of accounts. Changes can be made from time to time and new accounts can always be added, but it is difficult to make major changes to the account structure in the middle of the year—or even in subsequent years—without creating a lot of confusion and frustration.

In addition to recording financial transactions by account names and account numbers, we recommend that your press also account for these transactions by department (i.e., production; editorial; marketing and promotion; fund-raising; and management and general). This is especially the case when accounting for and tracking expenses. To add department codes, your press adds another tier to the chart of accounts. If your press uses department codes, they might look like the ones on page 29.

Figure 3-2
Chart
of Accounts:
Balance Sheet

Chart of Accounts: Balance Sheet

Account #	Account Description
1000	**ASSETS**
	Current Assets
1010	Cash—Checking
1020	Cash—Savings
1030	Investments
1040	Petty Cash
1210	Accounts Receivable
1220	Allowance for Doubtful Accounts
1230	Allowance for Sales Returns
1310	Grants and Contributions Receivable
1410	Author/Royalty Advances
1510	Inventory—Finished Books
1520	Inventory—Books in Process
1530	Allowance for Obsolete Inventory
1610	Prepaid Expenses
1620	Security Deposits
	TOTAL CURRENT ASSETS
	Fixed Assets
1710	Furniture & Fixtures
1720	Equipment
1730	Software
1740	Leasehold Improvements
1750	Accumulated Depreciation
1760	Accumulated Amortization
	TOTAL FIXED ASSETS
1810	Other Assets
	TOTAL ASSETS
2000	**LIABILITIES**
	Current Liabilities
2010	Accounts Payable
2110	Loans/Notes Payable
2120	Current Maturities—Long-Term Debt
2210	Accrued Salaries Payable
2220	FICA
2230	Federal Withholding
2240	State Withholding
2250	Retirement Funds Payable
2260	Other Accrued Payroll Taxes
2270	Accrued Vacation
2310	Royalties Payable
2410	Deferred Revenue
	TOTAL CURRENT LIABILITIES
	Long-Term Liabilities
2510	Long-Term Debt
2520	Capital Lease Payable
	TOTAL LONG-TERM LIABILITIES
	TOTAL LIABILITIES
3000	**NET ASSETS**
3110	Unrestricted Net Assets
3210	Temporarily Restricted Net Assets
3510	Current Year Surplus/(Deficit)
	TOTAL NET ASSETS
	TOTAL LIABILITIES AND NET ASSETS

Note: Line items without an account number represent subtotals and totals computed on actual financial statements.

Figure 3-3
Chart
of Accounts:
Statement
of Activities

Chart of Accounts: Statement of Activities

Account #	Account Description	Account #	Account Description
4000	**BOOK INCOME**	**6000 - 8000**	**OPERATING EXPENSES**
4010	Direct Sales	**6000**	**Personnel Costs**
4020	Distributor Sales	6010	Salaries
4030	Wholesale Sales	6020	Payroll Taxes
4110	(Discounts)	6030	Employee Benefits
4120	(Sales Returns)	**7000**	**General Expenses**
4130	(Returns Processing Fees)	7110	Professional Fees
4140	(Refunds)	7120	Outside Editorial Services
	NET SALES	7210	Supplies
4210	Subsidiary Rights Income	7220	Telephone
	TOTAL BOOK INCOME	7230	Postage and Shipping
		7240	Occupancy
5000	**COST OF BOOKS SOLD**	7250	Equipment Rental and Maintenance
	Inventory Beginning of Year	7260	Insurance
5010	Acquisition/Agent Fees	7270	Travel
5020	Permission Fees	7280	Trade Show Expense
5030	Rights Payments	7290	Advertising and Promotions
5040	Translation Fees	7310	Review Copies
5050	Cover Design/Artwork	7320	Catalog Expense
5060	Copyediting	7340	Other Fund-Raising Expenses
5070	Proofreading		
5080	Typesetting	7410	Employee Training
5090	Paper, Printing and Binding	7420	Conferences and Conventions
5110	Shipping	7610	Interest Expense
5120	Obsolete InventoryAdjustment	7710	Dues and Subscriptions
	Cost of Goods Available for Sale	7720	Bank Charges
	Less: Inventory End of Year	7730	Miscellaneous
	Total Production Costs	7840	Amortization
5210	Royalty Expense	7850	Depreciation
5220	Distribution Fees		**TOTAL OPERATING EXPENSES**
	TOTAL COST OF BOOKS SOLD		
			(LOSS FROM OPERATIONS)
	GROSS PROFIT		
			NET ASSETS RELEASED FROM RESTRICTIONS
		9000	**SUPPORT & OTHER INCOME**
		9010	Foundation Grants
		9050	Corporate Grants
		9110	Government Grants
		9150	Individual Contributions
		9210	Board Support
		9250	Sponsorships
		9310	In-Kind Contributions
		9410	Special Events Income
		9420	(Special Event Expenses)
		9510	Interest/Investment Income
		9610	Other Income
			TOTAL SUPPORT & OTHER INCOME
			SURPLUS (DEFICIT)

Note: Line items without an account number represent subtotals and totals computed on actual financial statements.

Department Codes

Cost of Books Sold	= 01
Production	= 02
Editorial	= 03
Marketing and Promotion	= 04
Fund-Raising	= 05
Management and General	= 06

Accordingly, when posting transactions, your bookkeeping forms would have a column each for the account and department numbers and would look something like this:

Account #   Department #
XXXX   XX

When a foundation or other donor contributes money to your press for a specific project or purpose, it is called a *restricted contribution*. At some point, outside donors will require a financial report that recaps how the funds were used. To track the receipt and disbursement of these contributed funds, we recommend that your press also establish codes for net asset classes (unrestricted, temporarily restricted or permanently restricted) in the chart of accounts. (These net asset classes will be discussed further in Chapter 5). This will require you to add a third tier to the chart of accounts, such as the following:

**Codes for
Net Asset Classes**

Unrestricted Contributions	= 100
Temporarily Restricted Contributions	= 200

Account #   Department #   Asset Class #
XXXX   XX   XXX

If your system allows, we recommend yet a fourth tier in your press's chart of accounts to allow you to track income and expenses by book. If your accounting system does not allow for tracking this information for each book, at a minimum, the expenses for each book must be detailed and accounted on a spreadsheet to allow you to determine the total cost to produce each book. You will need this information for each title in your inventory if you are to accurately account for inventory and the cost of books sold (see Chapter 7).

Account #   Department #   Asset Class #   Book #
XXXX   XX   XXX   XXXX

As you can see, a chart of accounts can be very simple or it can become quite complex by adding tiers such as departments, class and books. Within reason and with consideration given to the type of computers and accounting software your press uses, the more detailed your chart of accounts, the more financial information will be available to effectively manage the finances of your press. Greater detail in the chart of accounts can also save time, energy and headaches because it will enable your accounting system to produce certain financial reports that would otherwise need to be created on a spreadsheet by someone in your organization.

· ·

Registers, Journals and Ledgers

For every financial transaction, the detail from that transaction must be referenced or summarized in some type of record-keeping document. In accounting terms, these record-keeping documents or reports are called registers, journals and ledgers. Together these reports form a *set of books* for your organization. Whether you use a manual record-keeping system or a computerized one, the basic concepts of record keeping remain the same. Examples of the registers, journals and ledgers described below are included in the appendix section of this book.

Accounts Payable Register

Whenever the press receives a bill or invoice, it is posted to the *accounts payable register*—even if it is paid the same day it is received. Information that should be recorded for each bill or invoice in the register includes:

- the expense-account name and number from the chart of accounts to which the bill is being charged;
- the name of the vendor or creditor;
- the date of the invoice; and
- the amount of the invoice.

When recording a payment on an account in the payable register, you need to record the date of payment and the number of the check used to make the payment.

At the end of the month, all entries in the accounts payable register are totaled by account number. The total amount of accounts payable (all invoices recorded for that month) is posted, as a credit entry, increasing the accounts payable liability in the general ledger. Keep in mind that every accounting entry has two parts—a debit and a credit. Accordingly, the offset to the credit entry made to the accounts payable account is a debit entry to each expense account in the general ledger for all costs charged to it during the month.

Accounts Payable Subsidiary Ledger and Aging

A record must be kept of each vendor to whom money is owed. The place where this data is kept is called the *accounts payable subsidiary ledger*. In this ledger, you can also track how long each unpaid invoice has been outstanding. This is called *aging your payables* and is usually compiled in increments of 30 days.

When all of the *unpaid invoices* in this subsidiary ledger are totaled at the end of the month, the amount should equal the balance of the accounts payable account in the general ledger. If the two amounts are not equal, an error or mistake has been made and the bookkeeper or accountant needs to search for and correct the error(s) until the balances agree.

Cash Disbursements Journal

The *cash disbursements journal* is used to record all disbursements of funds— whether by check or cash (most will be by check). Information to be documented in this journal includes the date of the disbursement, the check number, to whom the check was written and the amount of the check. Disbursements for invoices recorded in the accounts payable register are recorded in this journal, as well as in the accounts payable register. At the end of the month, disbursements are totaled and a credit entry is made to the cash account, thereby reducing the assets balance in the general ledger. The offsetting debit entry is to reduce accounts payable, which is listed under liabilities in the general ledger.

Sales Register

The *sales register* is where your press accounts for book sales. Within reason, the greater the amount of detail documented in the press's sales register, the better able the press will be to make informed decisions about the books it ultimately publishes and where it sells them. Information obtained from a properly designed sales register should tell the press:

*   which books are selling and which are not;
*   where the books are sold (i.e., chain stores, independent bookstores, libraries, classrooms, individuals, etc.);
*   how the books are sold (i.e., direct, distributors, wholesalers, etc.); and
*   the amount of sales returns for each book.

While sophisticated computer software packages are available for tracking book sales and accounts receivable, the fact is that most small nonprofit presses cannot afford such software and must design and develop their own sales and accounts receivable tracking systems using database software. There is no standard method for creating databases to account for book sales data. Each press should carefully consider what and how much sales information it would like to track and design its own database accordingly.

Information to account for monthly sales will usually come from two sources: a distributor's monthly sales report and the press's monthly internal sales register for books it has sold directly. For books sold directly, the press is responsible for preparing invoices (creating a *receivable*) to be sent to the customer. For distributor sales, the distributor calculates and communicates a total amount due the press for each month.

At the end of the month, all of the direct sales posted to the sales register are totaled and combined with the totals from the distributor's monthly sales report. From these figures, the press prepares a journal entry to account for the sales activity. In its simplest form, the press credits the sales accounts and debits the accounts receivable account on the general ledger by the amounts of the total monthly sales in the sales registers.

Cash Receipts Journal

All cash received by the press should be recorded in a *cash receipts journal*. Any cash received that relates to book sales and represents payment for an invoice that was recorded in the sales register, increases cash and decreases accounts receivable. Any other cash received usually represents payment of some other type of income (i.e., a foundation grant, a contribution from an individual, payment for subsidiary rights, etc.). For these cash receipts, the name and number of the income account to which the amount will be posted should also be recorded in the cash receipts journal. All cash recorded in the cash receipts journal is totaled at the end of the month and this amount is posted as a debit to the cash account in the general ledger, increasing the cash balance. The offsetting credit entries will be made to the accounts receivable account and all other accounts listed in the journal.

Accounts Receivable Subsidiary Ledger and Aging

After posting a sale to the sales register, a corresponding entry should be posted to the customer's account in the accounts receivable subsidiary ledger. The *accounts receivable subsidiary ledger* keeps track of how much each customer owes your press, amounts paid on each account and how long each invoice has been outstanding. Any payments received from the customer, besides being recorded in the cash receipts journal, are also recorded to this subsidiary ledger.

At the end of the month, the total of all customer accounts in the accounts receivable subsidiary ledger should equal the balance in the general ledger's accounts receivable account. If the two amounts do not balance, an error(s) has been made and needs to be found and corrected to bring these two amounts into balance.

Perpetual Book Inventory Register

The *perpetual book inventory register* provides a means for tracking each title as it moves through your inventory. To make the most of this system, the costs associated with producing each book must be accounted for individually, either as part of the accounting system or on a separate spreadsheet. The perpetual inventory registers begin with an inventory of each title at the beginning of a period (both in number of books and dollar amount). As finished books are added to the inventory, number and cost of the books are added to the account. As books are removed from the inventory—either as books sold, complimentary copies, authors' copies or damaged books—they are subtracted from the account. Ending inventory for the period is determined by adding the dollar value of new stock to the beginning inventory value and then subtracting the value of books removed from the inventory.

Calculating Ending Book Inventory

		Number of Books	Dollar Value of Books
	Beginning Book Inventory	XXXXX	$ XXXXX
Plus:	Books Added to Inventory	XXXX	$ XXXX
	Books Available for Sale	XXXXX	$ XXXXX
Less:	Books Sold	(XXXX)	
	Complimentary Books	(XXX)	
	Books to Authors	(XX)	
	Damaged Books (Hurts)	(XX)	
	Number/Cost of Books Sold	(XXXX)	$ (XXXX)
Equals:	Ending Book Inventory	XXXXX	$ XXXXX

Alternatively, the value of the ending inventory may be calculated by multiplying the number of each title in stock by its unit value (the cost of producing each copy). The press's total ending inventory is determined by totaling the ending inventories for each title. (See Chapter 7 for more detail on the accounting and record-keeping processes for book inventory.)

Payroll Register

Payroll may be prepared as an internal function of the organization or it may be out-sourced to a payroll service. Regardless of which method the press uses, a *payroll register* must be maintained to keep track of each employee's gross salary, deductions and withholdings. At the end of each payroll or at the end of the month, entries are made to the appropriate general ledger accounts, recording all payroll activity for that period.

Many presses attempt to keep track of each employee's wages by hours worked in various departments or on specific projects. Accordingly, in addition to accounting for total salaries, the press will also know the personnel costs expended in each of its departments or for producing each title in its catalog.

General Journal

The *general journal* is where the press records financial transactions related to accounts that are not accounted for in the processes discussed above. These journal entries are necessary to provide a complete and accurate financial picture of your press. A small nonprofit press would typically use the general journal to record items such as:

- monthly depreciation expense;
- cost of books sold;
- accounts receivable that are deemed to be uncollectable (bad-debt losses);
- advances on authors' royalties (recorded as a prepaid expense here, and later used to calculate the cost of the finished book);
- confirmed foundation grants for which money has not yet been received (grants receivable);
- bank charges;
- interest income; and
- transfers between checking and savings accounts.

General Ledger

The *general ledger* is the accounting book or ledger that shows you, in one place, all the transactions, by amount and date, for each account listed in the chart of accounts. A new general ledger is started at the beginning of each fiscal year, with fund balances carried over from the end of the prior year. Activity recorded in the accounts payable register, cash disbursements journal, sales register, cash receipts journal, payroll register and general journal are added or subtracted from the appropriate accounts in the general ledger. The resulting totals provide ending balances for each account and these balances are then used in creating the financial statements. If you ever question the balance in an account, the place to start looking for the answers is the general ledger.

Trial Balance

The *trial balance* is a listing of every account in the general ledger, along with the balance of each account. These account balances are usually listed in two columns—as debits (on the left) and credits (on the right). If everything has been recorded and posted correctly, the debits and credits will equal each other. Once it is determined that the trial balance balances, financial statements can be prepared.

....

Summary

A good accounting system will provide you with information essential to the survival of your small press. Elements essential to a good accounting system are:

- accounting on the accrual basis;
- a double-entry system for recording all financial transactions;
- a comprehensive chart of accounts with the capacity to track financial information on different levels or tiers; and
- proper journals, registers and ledgers for providing documentation and support of all financial transactions.

Only with a complete set of books will you be able to evaluate the business operations of your press, make changes as needed and plan for the future.

chapter 4

Pulling It All Together With Financial Statements

Chapter Highlights

▶ Determining Your Net Worth: The Balance Sheet

▶ Tracking Income and Expenses: The Statement of Activities

▶ Departmental Functions of a Nonprofit Press

▶ Deciphering the Numbers: Financial Analysis

▶ Balance Sheet Ratios

▶ Statement of Activities Ratios

▶ Interstatement Ratios

▶ Beyond the Calculations

Pulling It All Together
With Financial Statements

The previous chapter discussed both the processes and the documents your press needs to accurately account for its day-to-day financial transactions. The next step is to consolidate all the data from the journals, registers and ledgers into *financial statements*. Financial statements are the summary products of the accounting process. When properly prepared and presented, financial statements provide the reader with the information necessary to make financial decisions.

Your accounting system should be designed in such a way that the resulting financial statements meet the needs of both internal and external decision makers. Internal decision makers consist of your press's management and board of directors. For the internal audience, you are allowed a certain degree of flexibility and freedom as to what financial information is included in the statements and in how it is prepared and presented. External users usually require more formal financial information prepared in accordance with generally accepted accounting principles.

This chapter describes the basic financial statements your small nonprofit press will prepare *internally* on a monthly basis and the components within these statements. The intent of this chapter is to introduce you to general financial statement concepts and content. In later chapters we will discuss the accounting concepts and procedures required for *external* financial statements.

For internal purposes, a small nonprofit press will typically produce two financial statements on a monthly basis: a *balance sheet* and a *statement of activities*, also called a *profit and loss statement* or the *income statement*.

Determining Your Net Worth: The Balance Sheet

In one concise statement, the balance sheet shows your press's financial position. It tells at a particular point in time what your press owns, what it owes and the difference between these two amounts—or the press's net worth. The accounting equation that gives the balance sheet its title is:

$$Assets = Liabilities + Net\ Assets.$$

Each term in this equation has a specific meaning:

- **Assets** are the economic resources your press *owns* or to which it has claim. Your press's assets will most likely include cash, accounts receivable, grants receivable, inventory, prepaid expenses, royalty advances and equipment.

  Assets can be classified as either *current* or *noncurrent.* Current assets include those accounts that can reasonably be expected to be turned into cash or consumed within a year. Noncurrent assets for most small nonprofit presses include property, such as furniture and equipment, that is not easily converted to cash or which has a useful life of several years. Noncurrent assets might also include investments, buildings and grants scheduled to be received sometime after the next 12 months.

- **Liabilities** are financial obligations—or money the press *owes* to others. Your press's liabilities probably include accounts payable, accrued expenses like salaries, payroll taxes and royalties, and notes or loans payable. Similar to assets, liabilities may also be classified as current (those obligations due within one year) or noncurrent (debts due beyond one year).

- **Net Assets** (previously known in the nonprofit sector as *fund balance*) is the difference between total assets (what the press owns) and total liabilities (what it owes). Net assets represents the accumulation of surpluses or deficits your press has achieved since it began operating. If, through the years, surpluses have exceeded deficits, net assets will be a positive amount. If the opposite has occurred, your press will show a negative net worth and could be in financial trouble. Net assets is the equivalent of owner's equity or net worth in a commercial enterprise.

A typical balance sheet for a small nonprofit press will look similar to the one shown in Figure 4-1 (page 38).

Figure 4-1

Sample
Balance Sheet

Sample Balance Sheet
June 30, 19XX

ASSETS		LIABILITIES AND NET ASSETS	
Current Assets:		**Current Liabilities:**	
Cash—Checking	$ 5,000	Accounts Payable	$ 45,000
Cash—Savings	10,000	Loans Payable	20,000
Petty Cash	100	Current Portion of Capital	
Accounts Receivable—Distributor	50,000	Lease Payable	2,000
Less: Allowance for Sales Returns	(10,000)	Accrued Salaries Payable	6,000
Accounts Receivable—Direct	8,000	Payroll Taxes Accrued	
Less: Allowance for Doubtful Accounts	(400)	and Withheld	1,000
Grants Receivable—Unrestricted	10,000	Royalties Payable	15,000
Grants Receivable—			
Temporarily Restricted	20,000	**Total Current Liabilities**	**89,000**
Inventory	150,000		
Allowance for Obsolete Inventory	(22,000)	**Long-Term Liabilities:**	
Royalty Advances	3,000	Capital Lease Payable	8,000
Prepaid Expenses	1,000	**Total Long-Term Liabilities**	**8,000**
Total Current Assets	**224,700**	**Total Liabilities**	**97,000**
Fixed Assets:		**NET ASSETS:**	
Furniture & Equipment	30,000	Unrestricted Net Assets—	
Leasehold Improvements	5,000	Beginning of Year	120,000
Computer Software	10,000	Current Year Surplus/	
Less: Accumulated Depreciation	(15,000)	(Deficit)	7,700
Less: Accumulated Amortization	(6,000)	Unrestricted Net Assets—	
		End of Year	127,700
Total Fixed Assets	**24,000**		
		Temporarily Restricted Net	
Other Assets	**1,000**	Assets—Beginning of Year	20,000
		Current Year Surplus/(Deficit)	5,000
Total Assets	**$249,700**	Temporarily Restricted Net	
		Assets—End of Year	25,000
		Total Net Assets	**152,700**
		Total Liabilities and	
		Net Assets	**$249,700**

Tracking Income and Expenses: The Statement of Activities

The statement of activities is the financial statement that shows all of your press's financial activities from the beginning to the end of the fiscal year. This statement shows where your income came from, where it was spent and how much you had left (surplus) or were short (deficit) at the end of the year. A typical statement of activities for a small nonprofit press includes year-to-date activity from book sales, cost of books sold, subsidiary rights sales, contributed and other income, expenses from program services and expenses from support services.

Currently, there is no standard in the small press industry, nor in the accounting profession, for how information in the statement of activities should be presented. This causes a problem when it comes to comparing the financial operations of two or more small nonprofit presses. Not only is there no consistency of format for these statements, in many instances what is contained in certain line items—specifically, cost of books sold—also varies from press to press.

A primary objective of this financial handbook is to recommend a statement of activities reporting format so that most, if not all, small nonprofit presses are reporting the results of their financial operations in a similar and consistent manner. Accordingly, we recommend the format pictured in Figure 4-2 (page 40) as a "universal" statement of activities format for small nonprofit presses.

For internal purposes, the statement of activities should not only show actual revenues and expenses, but also comparisons of the actual amounts with the budgeted amounts (Figure 4-3, pages 42 and 43). This can be done for each month (current-month actual amounts compared with current-month budgeted amounts) and for year-to-date amounts (year-to-date actual amounts compared to year-to-date budgeted amounts). By including budgeted amounts in the statement of activities and analyzing the differences (variances) between budgeted and actual, you now have a financial tool that helps you see if you are on track with your financial plan. This information then enables you to make informed decisions on what changes, if any, need to be made to your financial operations. If the financial statements are prepared in a timely fashion and if the information from them is used properly, you have the opportunity to be proactive, rather then reactive, with your management decisions.

Figure 4-2

Sample
Statement
of Activities—
Condensed Version

Sample Statement of Activities—Condensed Version
For the Period Ending June 30, 19XX

	Unrestricted	Temporarily Restricted	Total
OPERATING REVENUE			
Distributor Sales, Net of Discounts and Returns	$250,000		$250,000
Press Sales, Net of Discounts and Returns	30,000		30,000
Total Book Sales Revenue	280,000	0	280,000
Rights Income	15,000		15,000
Total Operating Revenue	295,000	0	295,000
COST OF BOOKS SOLD			
Cost of Books Sold	118,000		118,000
Royalties Expense	20,000		20,000
Distribution Expense	60,000		60,000
Total Cost of Books Sold	198,000	0	198,000
GROSS PROFIT FROM BOOK SALES	97,000	0	97,000
OPERATING EXPENSES			
Program Services:			
Production	30,000		30,000
Editorial	45,000		45,000
Marketing and Promotion	95,000		95,000
Total Program Services	170,000	0	170,000
Support Services:			
Management and General	60,000		60,000
Fund-Raising	25,000		25,000
Total Support Services	85,000	0	85,000
Total Operating Expenses	255,000	0	255,000
Deficit From Operations	(158,000)	0	(158,000)
SUPPORT AND OTHER INCOME			
Contributions	63,700	90,000	153,700
Net Assets Released from Restrictions:			
—Satisfaction of Program Restrictions	65,000	(65,000)	0
—Expiration of Time Restrictions	20,000	(20,000)	0
Special Events (net)	15,000		15,000
Interest Income	1,000		1,000
Other Income	1,000	0	1,000
Total Support and Other Income	165,700	5,000	170,700
CHANGE IN NET ASSETS	$7,700	5,000	$12,700

Departmental Functions of a Nonprofit Press

If you are like many people in the small nonprofit arena, it's quite possible that you think of your press's activities as one big operation, without delineating the financial activities by their functions. But even the simplest small press has "departments" or *functions* into which all expenses can be categorized. The box below describes the departmental functions within the typical nonprofit press.

Cost of Books Sold—Cost of books sold includes services and activities directly related to the production of books, including acquisition costs, production, typesetting, printing, warehousing, distribution and payment of royalties.

Production—Production includes salaries of employees involved in the book-production process, associated occupancy office costs and other incidental costs related to production, but not specifically identifiable to a particular book.

Editorial—Editorial services include developing manuscripts and preparing them for publication, cultivating authors and creating and maintaining a presence within the editorial segment of the publishing industry.

Marketing and Promotion—Marketing and promotion activities include advertising, marketing, public relations and outreach to schools, libraries, the book trade and individuals.

Management and General—Management and general functions include those services and activities performed that support the operations of the press, but are not identified with a particular cost-of-books-sold, production, editorial or marketing and promotion function. Management and general expenses are often thought to be more administrative in nature and might include items like legal and accounting costs and board of directors meeting expenses.

Fund-Raising—Fund-raising includes those costs associated with raising contributed dollars and is often thought of as development costs.

Although tracking departmental or function expenses may be more detailed and time consuming than you require for daily operations, such tracking may be necessary if your press is to pass its annual audit or for filing the IRS Form 990. Even if you choose a less-detailed accounting system, it is important that you accurately separate *program* costs (all expenses related to the cost of books sold, production, editorial, marketing and promotion functions) from the costs involved in management and fund-raising (*support* expenses).

Figure 4-3
Internal
Statement
of Activities
Format With
Actual-to-Budget
Comparisons

Internal Statement of Activities (with budget comparisons)
For the Period Ended _____, _____

	Current Month			Year To-Date			Annual Budget
	Actual	Budget	Variance	Actual	Budget	Variance	
Book Income							
Direct Sales	$	$	$	$	$	$	$
Distributor Sales							
Wholesale Sales							
(Discounts)							
(Sales Returns)							
(Returns/ Processing Fees)							
(Refunds)							
Net Sales							
Subsidiary Rights Income							
Total Book Income							
Cost of Books Sold							
Inventory Beginning of Period							
Acquisition/Agent Fees							
Permission Fees							
Rights Payments							
Translation Fees							
Cover Design/Artwork							
Copyediting							
Proofreading							
Typesetting							
Paper, Printing, Binding							
Shipping							
Obsolete Inventory Adjustment							
Cost of Books Available for Sale							
Less: Inventory End of Period							
Total Production Costs							
Royalty Expense							
Distribution Fees							
Total Cost of Books Sold							
Gross Profit	$	$	$	$	$	$	$

(continued)

Figure 4-3
Internal
Statement
of Activities
Format With
Actual-to-Budget
Comparisons
(continued)

Internal Statement of Activities (with budget comparisons)
For the Period Ended _____, _____

	Current Month			Year To-Date			Annual Budget
	Actual	Budget	Variance	Actual	Budget	Variance	
Operating Expenses							
Salaries	$	$	$	$	$	$	$
Payroll Taxes							
Employee Benefits							
Professional Fees							
Outside Editorial Services							
Supplies							
Telephone							
Postage and Shipping							
Occupancy							
Equipment Rental and Maintenance							
Insurance							
Travel							
Trade Show Expense							
Advertising and Promotions							
Review Copies							
Catalog Expense							
Other Fund-Raising Expense							
Employee Training							
Conferences and Conventions							
Interest Expense							
Dues and Subscriptions							
Bank Charges							
Miscellaneous							
Amortization							
Depreciation							
Total Operating Expenses							
(Deficit from Operations)							
Support & Other Income							
Foundation Grants							
Corporate Grants							
Government Grants							
Individual Contributions							
Board Support							
Sponsorships							
In-Kind Contributions							
Special Events Income							
(Special Event Expenses)							
Interest Income							
Other Income							
Total Support & Other Income							
Change in Net Assets	$	$	$	$	$	$	$

Deciphering the Numbers: Financial Analysis

Once the internal financial statements have been prepared, you are ready to put them to full use. *Ratio analysis* is the financial management technique that allows you to interpret your press's financial condition using designated financial indicators.

Ratios can be used to measure relationships among amounts on the balance sheet (balance sheet ratios), among amounts on the statement of activities (statement of activity ratios) or between amounts from both of these statements (interstatement ratios). A number of ratios can be used when interpreting financial data, but your press should focus only on those that have the potential of shedding additional light on your press's financial situation. Below is a discussion of those ratios that have particular significance for most nonprofit presses. (Note: The numbers used in the examples below come from the sample balance sheet and statement of activities presented in Figures 4-1 and 4-2, pages 38 and 40. To make these examples come alive, you may want to refer back to those earlier figures.)

....

Balance Sheet Ratios

Current Ratio

The *current ratio* is calculated by dividing your press's *current assets* (those assets that can be expected to be turned to cash or consumed within a year) by its current liabilities (those obligations due within one year). A current ratio with a value of 1 or more is considered good, as this indicates that your press has resources available to meet its current obligations. A value of less than 1 indicates that the current obligations of your press exceed the resources currently available and your press could have a liquidity problem. Liquidity is the most fundamental measurement of financial stability. In the example below, the current ratio of 2.53 means the press has $2.53 in current assets for each dollar of current liabilities.

$$\frac{\text{Current Assets}}{\text{Current Liabilities}} = \frac{\$224,700}{\$89,000} = 2.53$$

Quick Ratio

The *quick ratio*, like the current ratio, also measures liquidity. The quick ratio, however, only takes into consideration those current assets held as cash and those that can quickly be converted to cash (i.e., accounts receivable). Less-liquid assets like inventory and prepaid expenses are left out of the equation. The result is a more fine-tuned and conservative measurement of liquidity. In the example from above, the amount of cash and accounts receivable available to cover every dollar of current liabilities has now been reduced to $0.70 when measured by the quick ratio.

$$\frac{\text{Cash} + \text{Total Accounts Receivable}}{\text{Current Liabilities}} = \frac{\$15,100 + \$47,600}{\$89,000} = \frac{\$62,700}{\$89,000} = 0.70$$

**Cash On Hand
to Current
Liabilities**

The *cash on hand to current liabilities* ratio is even more conservative than the quick ratio in that it only measures your press's ability to meet *current obligations* with the actual cash on hand. This ratio is probably more useful to your press than the current or quick ratios for two reasons. First, most small presses have a substantial amount of assets tied up in inventory. Second, there is a good chance that most of the press's accounts receivable balance represents amounts due from a distributor, which means that full payment on those receivables may not be received for another three or four months. For these two reasons, your press's ability to maintain enough cash on hand to meet its current obligations becomes an ongoing concern. Therefore, attention to this ratio should play a priority in the financial management of your press. In our example, the cash on hand to current liabilities ratio indicates that the press only has $0.17 in cash to cover every dollar of its current obligations. Although not a healthy one, this tends to be a common situation for most nonprofit presses.

$$\frac{\text{Total Cash}}{\text{Current Liabilities}} = \frac{\$15,100}{\$89,000} = 0.17$$

**Debt to
Net Assets**

The *debt to net assets* ratio is determined by dividing your press's total loan and notes payable debt by its total net assets. The measurement here is to see how much of the press's net assets or net worth is comprised of debt. The higher the percentage, the more the organization relies on borrowed money for its ongoing operations. Borrowing money is not necessarily bad for your press. A large amount of your press's working capital is likely to be tied up in inventory and receivables, leaving you no alternative but to borrow money for ongoing operations. On the other hand, the fact that your press has debt is all the more reason to monitor the collections of your receivables and to maintain inventory levels that are adequate to meet sales, but not so large that they drain the press of operating cash. In our example, 19.65 percent of the press's net worth is made up of debt in the form of a loan and a capital lease payable. This is an acceptable percentage; however, the cash on hand to current liabilities ratio above indicates that the press may need to borrow more money to pay its current obligations. Doing so would in turn increase the press's debt to net asset ratio.

$$\frac{\text{Loans and Notes Payable}}{\text{Net Assets}} = \frac{\$\ 30,000}{\$152,700} = 19.65\%$$

**Statement
of Activities
Ratios**

The *gross profit percentage* is calculated by dividing your press's gross profit from book sales (total book sales minus total cost of books sold) by its total book sales. The resulting percentage provides two valuable pieces of information. First, it tells you how much of every dollar of book sales was needed to pay for the cost of producing the books that were sold. Second, it tells you

Gross Profit Percentage

how much of every dollar of books sold is leftover to cover the press's general operating expenses. In our example, the press has earned $0.33 on every dollar of book sales. Or put another way, $0.67 of every dollar of book sales was used to cover the direct cost of the books.

$$\frac{\text{Gross Profit From Book Sales}}{\text{Total Book Sales (including Rights Income)}} = \frac{\$\ 97,000}{\$295,000} = 33\%$$

Contributed vs. Book Sales Income

Knowing what percentage of your press's income comes from *book sales* and what percentage comes from *contributed income* is important for managing your press. Given that the main focus of your press is to produce and sell books and given the uncertainty of your press's ability to raise contributions, the higher the percentage of book sales income, the better off your press is. In the example below, contributed income represents 36 percent of the press's total income, while income from book sales provides 64 percent of the press's total income.

$$\frac{\text{Contributed Income}}{\text{Total Income}} = \frac{\$163,700}{\$460,700} = 36\% \quad \frac{\text{Book Sales Income}}{\text{Total Income}} = \frac{\$295,000}{\$460,700} = 64\%$$

Most individuals or organizations contributing money to your press will expect the money to be used to support the press's programs. Because of this, it is imperative that your press use a majority of contributed funds for their program purpose—not on management and general (administrative) or fund-raising expenses.

Program vs. Operating Expenses

By calculating the percentages of *program expenses to total expenses* and *fund-raising/management expenses to total expenses*, your press has a barometer with which to measure how much it is spending in these areas. A rule of thumb to follow is that at least 70 percent of the total expenses of your press must be used to support its programs. The higher this percentage, the better. The results of these ratios in our example indicate that the press is spending 81 percent of all of its expenses on its programs and the remaining 19 percent is being expended on management and general and fund-raising expenses or support services.

Program to Total Expense Ratio

$$\frac{\text{COBS + Program Services Expenses}}{\text{COBS + Total Operating Expenses}} = \frac{\$198,000 + \$170,000}{\$198,000 + \$255,000} = \frac{\$368,000}{\$453,000} = 81\%$$

Fund-Raising and Management to Total Expense Ratio

$$\frac{\text{Total Support Services}}{\text{COBS + Total Operating Expenses}} = \frac{\$\ 85,000}{\$198,000 + \$255,000} = \frac{\$\ 85,000}{\$453,000} = 19\%$$

Interstatement Ratios

The next three *interstatement ratios,* more than any of those previously discussed, are representative of the fact that your press is a business that produces and sells books. To many other nonprofit organizations these ratios either do not apply or have very little meaning. It is important to compute these ratios and understand what they mean so you can use them to enhance the financial decision making of your press. For the most part, these three ratios are only calculated at the *end of your press's fiscal year*, while the balance sheet and statement of activity ratios discussed above can be used at any time during the year.

Accounts Receivable Turnover

The *accounts receivable turnover ratio* is derived by dividing total book sales for the year by the average accounts receivable balance between the beginning and the end of the fiscal year. The higher the turnover of receivables during the year, the shorter the time between sales and cash collection. In our example, the balance in accounts receivable has turned over, or recycled, 5.88 times in the past year (using an end-of-year-only accounts receivable balance). This ratio by itself does not mean much; however, when compared to the same ratio computed in prior years or to an industry average for this ratio, your press has a better barometer for determining whether or not it is collecting money owed to it in a timely fashion.

$$\frac{\text{Total Book Sales}}{\text{Accounts Receivable}} = \frac{\$280,000}{\$47,600} = 5.88$$

Days Accounts Receivable Outstanding

The *days accounts receivables outstanding ratio* is calculated by dividing the average of your press's outstanding accounts receivable balance between the beginning of the year and the end of the year by total book sales for the year and then multiplying the result times 365 days. The final result tells you the average number of days your accounts receivable are outstanding. The reason for computing this ratio is that the faster your collection time, the more cash you have on hand with which to operate! The example below computes this press's outstanding accounts receivable average at 62 days (using an end-of-year-only accounts receivable balance). Again, by comparing the results of this ratio to those of prior years or industry standards, you are better able to tell if your press is collecting accounts within a reasonable amount of time. Questions you might want to ask yourself include: Is 62 days a long time for a receivable to be outstanding? Can steps be taken to decrease the number of days a receivable is outstanding, thereby giving us more cash to operate with on a day-to-day basis?

$$\frac{\text{Accounts Receivable}}{\text{Total Book Sales}} = \frac{\$47,600}{\$280,000} = 0.17 \times 365 \text{ days} = 62.05$$

Inventory Turnover

The *inventory turnover ratio* measures how quickly your press is selling its inventory. The ratio is calculated by dividing the cost of books sold for the fiscal year by the average amount of inventory between the beginning and the end of the fiscal year.

In the example below, the inventory has turned 1.55 times in the past year. The higher this ratio is, the more books you are selling or the faster you are getting your books out of inventory. If your press has a significant amount of inventory in backlist titles that are not selling fast, the inventory turnover ratio will probably be low. This ratio really makes you think about your inventory levels and whether steps need to be taken to reduce them. Again, use past years' ratios or industry standards to help you gauge the health of your inventory turnover.

$$\frac{\text{Cost of Books Sold}}{\text{Inventory}} = \frac{\$198,000}{\$128,000} = 1.55$$

Beyond the Calculations

Preparing and calculating each of the above ratios is only the first step in the ratio-analysis process. Other procedures include:

- understanding and interpreting what each of the ratios means about the press's financial operations;

- comparing the ratios prepared using your press's most recent financial information with those of previous months or years; and

- comparing your press's ratios to those of other small nonprofit presses or to ratios for the small nonprofit industry as a whole.

Ratios provide a different perspective for analyzing your press's financial information and have the potential of giving meaningful insight into the well-being of your press. Usually one ratio alone does not offer reliable insight, but when an integrated package of ratios is prepared and analyzed, the picture of financial health that is painted can be quite revealing. By comparing significant ratios over multiple periods of time, you give yourself a valuable tool to evaluate your press's progress, financial improvement or deterioration.

chapter 5

New Standards
for Nonprofit Accounting

Chapter Highlights

▶ **New Accounting Standards**

▶ **FASB No. 117: Nonprofit Financial Statements**

▶ **FASB No. 116: Accounting for Contributions**

▶ **Defining Conditional, Unconditional and Restricted Contributions**

▶ **Reporting Conditional Contributions**

▶ **Accounting for Contributed Services**

New Standards
for Nonprofit Accounting

Just as commercial publishing houses and nonprofit literary presses differ in their purposes for existing, they also differ in the way they account for their respective financial resources. The primary reason for these differences is that nonprofit, tax-exempt organizations generally receive contributions or grants from foundations, corporations, governmental agencies and the general public, while commercial businesses do not. Because donors of these contributed resources often place restrictions on how or when their funds can be used by the organization, nonprofit organizations are responsible for detailed accounting and stewardship of these funds. In many cases, nonprofits must report back to granting agencies on disposition of these restricted funds.

Over the years, the accounting profession has developed accounting standards specifically for nonprofit organizations. These separate standards pertain to the proper accounting treatment of certain transactions unique to nonprofit organizations and to how information is presented in the financial statements. As this handbook goes to press, the accounting standards for nonprofit organizations are in a state of transition.

New Accounting Standards

In 1993, the Financial Accounting Standards Board (FASB), after 10 years of planning and development, issued two new Statements of Financial Accounting Standards (SFAS) for nonprofits. These statements—*FASB Statement No. 116, "Accounting for Contributions Received and Contributions Made,"* and *FASB Statement No. 117, "Financial Statements of Not-for-Profit Organizations"* (sometimes referred to as FASB 116 and FASB 117, respectively)—made major changes to the way nonprofit organizations account for contributions and report their financial information. As a result of these new standards, most small nonprofit presses will be required to make changes in their accounting formats and practices beginning in fiscal year 1996.

Perhaps the biggest change brought about by these standards is the elimination of *fund accounting*. Fund accounting classified nonprofits' resources into funds according to their nature, purpose or restrictions, if any. A fund was thought of as its own accounting entity, usually with a separate set of accounts maintained for each fund. For reporting purposes, those funds with similar characteristics were combined into fund groups. Fund groups commonly used by nonprofit organizations included:

- unrestricted;
- restricted;
- equipment;
- board designated; and
- endowment funds.

With the new FASB standards, the practice of fund accounting for external financial statements no longer exists. Instead, nonprofits are now required to organize and account for financial information using *net asset classes*. A key point to remember is that the new accounting standards, described below, apply only to *external financial reporting* (i.e., audited financial statements); many nonprofits may choose to continue using fund accounting for record keeping and internal reporting.

Why the Change?

Just when many small nonprofit presses were beginning to understand the concept of fund accounting, along came FASB 116 and 117. The main reason for the changes was the vast degree of inconsistency in the ways in which the various nonprofits accounted for contributions and presented information on their financial statements. In an effort to correct these inconsistencies, FASB issued the new accounting standards to enhance the relevance, clarity and comparability of financial statements issued by all nonprofit organizations.

All nonprofit organizations—including your press—must comply with these new accounting standards *if they receive contributions from outside donors*. The following two sections explain the new requirements and offer insight into the decisions your press's management will have to make as it implements these standards. Because FASB 116 is more technical in nature, we describe FASB 117 first.

· ·

FASB No. 117: Nonprofit Financial Statements

FASB 117 defines what information *must* be included on a nonprofit's financial statements and how this information may be displayed. But before your nonprofit press delves into the what's and how's of this statement, it needs to become familiar with the three net asset classes your press is now required to use in reporting its resources. The purpose of the three classes is to delineate assets with *donor-imposed restrictions* from those available for general use as the organization sees fit. The three classes are as follows:

Net Asset Classifications

- **Unrestricted Net Assets** are those assets unencumbered by donor restrictions and thus available for general use by the nonprofit;

- **Temporarily Restricted Net Assets** are the contributions received by a nonprofit with donor restrictions that will eventually expire or will be fulfilled by an action of the organization; and

- **Permanently Restricted Net Assets** are those contributed resources upon which the donor has placed a restriction that will never expire.

Net assets of the two restricted classes are created only by donor-imposed restrictions on their use. All other assets, including board-designated amounts, are legally considered unrestricted and must be reported as part of the unrestricted class. Examples of temporarily restricted net assets would be contributions that the donor has restricted for a specific use or ones that have been pledged, but will not be received until after the current year. An example of a permanently restricted net asset would be a large amount of money or piece of property that was donated for the purpose of generating investment income for the organization. Though the donor may stipulate that this investment may not be liquidated (sold or cashed in), any interest or other income earned from it would be available for use as unrestricted revenues.

Audit Requirements

In addition to the change in classification of net assets on the financial statements, FASB 117 also delineates the financial statements to be included as part of an audit and the types of information they are to contain. The following statements are those now required for an audit:

- a balance sheet;
- statement of activities;
- cash flow statement;
- accompanying notes to the financial statements; and
- a statement of functional expenses (recommended, not required).

Balance Sheet

Figure 5-1 presents a sample balance sheet using the new FASB format. FASB 117 requires nonprofit organizations to present information about the "liquidity" of their financial position. Providing this information tells the balance sheet's readers if your press will have enough cash in the near future to pay its bills as they come due. Liquidity information may be displayed in one or more of the following ways:

- sequencing assets and liabilities according to nearness of conversion to cash and use of cash, respectively;

- classifying assets and liabilities as *current* and *noncurrent* (this is often called a *classified balance sheet*)—we recommend that your press follow this method; or

- inclusion of disclosures regarding liquidity, including restrictions on use of assets, in the notes to the financial statements.

Figure 5-1

Balance Sheet
in Compliance With
FASB #117

**Balance Sheet
June 30, 19XX**

	Unrestricted	Temporarily Restricted	Total
ASSETS			
Current Assets:			
Cash	$ 10,100	$ 5,000	$ 15,100
Accounts Receivable (Less Allowance for Bad Debts and Returns of $10,400)	47,600		47,600
Grants and Contributions Receivable	10,000	20,000	30,000
Royalty Advances	3,000		3,000
Inventory (Less Allowance for Obsolescence of $22,000)	128,000		128,000
Prepaid Expenses	1,000		1,000
Total Current Assets	199,700	25,000	224,700
Equipment and Leasehold Improvements—Net	24,000		24,000
Other Assets	1,000		1,000
Total Assets	$224,700	$ 25,000	$249,700
LIABILITIES AND NET ASSETS			
Current Liabilities:			
Notes Payable	$ 20,000		$ 20,000
Current Maturities of Capital Lease Obligations	2,000		2,000
Accounts Payable	45,000		45,000
Accrued Salaries Payable	6,000		6,000
Payroll Taxes Accrued and Withheld	1,000		1,000
Royalties Payable	15,000		15,000
Total Current Liabilities	89,000	0	89,000
Long-Term Liabilities:			
Capital Lease Payable	8,000		8,000
Total Long-Term Liabilities	8,000		8,000
Total Liabilities	97,000	0	97,000
Net Assets:			
Unrestricted	127,700		127,700
Temporarily Restricted:			
For Support of Marketing and Promotion		5,000	5,000
For Use in Future Years	0	20,000	20,000
Total Net Assets	127,700	25,000	152,700
Total Liabilities and Net Assets	$224,700	$ 25,000	$249,700

Statement of Activities

Under FASB 117, your press has a great deal of flexibility in how it chooses to show its revenues and expenses on its statement of activities. A discussion on a recommended format for your press's statement of activities will follow, but first here is a listing of some of the requirements for this statement under FASB 117:

• Unless a donor explicitly stipulates a restriction, all contributions are considered to be unrestricted.

• Any income earned from temporarily or permanently restricted net assets will increase unrestricted net assets, unless donors or the law specifically restrict the use.

• If the stipulations of restricted contributions are met in the current reporting period, your press may report these contributions as unrestricted, provided this practice is consistently followed and disclosed in the notes.

• All expenses are reported as decreases in unrestricted net assets.

• Items that simultaneously increase one class of net assets and decrease another must be reported as a reclassification, which is reported separately from revenues, expenses, gains and losses. When this occurs, the amounts should be reported in a line item called "contributions (or net assets) released from restrictions" on the statement of activities.

• The new standard permits, but does not require, a distinction between operating and nonoperating items on the statement of activities.

The flexibility your press is allowed under FASB 117 comes in how it chooses to format its statement of activities. Your press's board, management, CPA and others having an interest in the statement of activities should work together to develop a format that will be most useful and understandable to those who will read and use the financial statements. The format we recommend is presented in Figure 5-2.

FASB No. 116: Accounting for Contributions

The complexities of FASB 116 alluded to earlier have to do with new classifications and accounting requirements for contributions. FASB established these new classifications and requirements to bring consistency to the way in which nonprofits account for contributions both received and made. The leadership of any press that supports its book sales through contributions from foundations or private donors must have at least a basic understanding of the terminology and content of FASB 116.

Understanding these new definitions and terms is important for several reasons. First, if you have a transaction that does not meet the definition of a contribution, the transaction falls outside the scope of FASB 116 and accordingly, the requirements under FASB 116 do not apply to that particular

Figure 5-2
Statement of
Activities in
Compliance With
FASB #117

Statement of Activities
For the Year Ended June 30, 19XX

	Unrestricted	Temporarily Restricted	Total
OPERATING REVENUE			
Book Sales—Net of Discounts and Returns	$280,000		$280,000
Rights Revenue	15,000		15,000
Total Operating Revenue	**295,000**	**0**	**295,000**
COST OF BOOKS SOLD			
Direct Costs of Books Sold	118,000		118,000
Royalties Expense	20,000		20,000
Distribution Expense	60,000		60,000
Total Cost of Books Sold	**198,000**	**0**	**198,000**
GROSS PROFIT FROM BOOK SALES	**97,000**		**97,000**
OPERATING EXPENSES			
Program Services:			
Production	30,000		30,000
Editorial	45,000		45,000
Marketing and Promotion	95,000		95,000
Total Program Services	**170,000**	**0**	**170,000**
Support Services:			
Management and General	60,000		60,000
Fund-Raising	25,000		25,000
Total Support Services	**85,000**	**0**	**85,000**
Total Operating Expenses	**255,000**	**0**	**255,000**
DEFICIT FROM OPERATIONS	**(158,000)**	**0**	**(158,000)**
Contributions Released from Restrictions:			
Satisfaction of Program Restrictions	65,000	(65,000)	0
Expiration of Time Restrictions	20,000	(20,000)	0
Total Net Assets Released from Restrictions	**85,000**	**(85,000)**	**0**
SUPPORT & OTHER INCOME:			
Contributions	48,700	90,000	138,700
In-Kind Contributions	15,000		15,000
Special Events	35,000		35,000
Special Events Costs	(20,000)		(20,000)
Interest/Investment Income	1,000		1,000
Other Income	1,000		1,000
Total Nonoperating Revenue	**80,700**	**90,000**	**170,700**
CHANGE IN NET ASSETS	**$ 7,700**	**$ 5,000**	**$ 12,700**

transaction. Second, with all nonprofit organizations using the same definitions, you will now be able to more accurately compare your press's financial performance with that of other nonprofit small presses, not only in the area of operations, but also in contributions and fund-raising.

．．

Defining Conditional, Unconditional and Restricted Contributions

Contribution—A transfer of cash or other assets (or a "promise to give" cash or other assets) to another entity in which the transfer or promise to give is unconditional, made or received voluntarily and is nonreciprocal.

Unconditional—A contribution where no strings are attached. Your press receives the contribution without having to first satisfy any conditions.

Nonreciprocal—Sources of cash or other assets for which the resource provider receives no value in exchange for the money provided.

Exchange Transactions—Examples of exchange (reciprocal) transactions include book sales, certain government grants (i.e., fee for service), membership dues and sponsorships. Cases in which something of value is exchanged for cash provided to the organization are considered reciprocal transactions and do not fall under the definition of a contribution. Therefore, all revenues from book sales or other service fees, membership dues and sponsorships are not contributions and not subject to new FASB requirements.

Promise to Give—A written or oral agreement to contribute cash or other assets to another entity. A promise to give (sometimes referred to as a "pledge") must contain sufficient verifiable documentation that a promise was made and received.

As you'll notice from the definitions, not only must your press account for (recognize) all contributions it receives, it must also recognize pledges for unconditional contributions that won't be received until a later date. These future contributions are posted as a "temporarily restricted contributions receivable." Here's an example: A foundation notifies you that it has approved a three-year $60,000 grant ($20,000 per year) to your press. Even though your press will only receive $20,000 in the current year, the entire $60,000 must be recorded as income in the year the award notification was received. The remaining $40,000 would be posted to the contributions receivable accounts under "temporarily restricted" class.

Not only must your press be able to recognize a contribution when it receives one, it also needs to be able to identify what kind of contribution it is. Under FASB 116, contributions are further broken down into four types:

• unrestricted and unconditional contributions;
• restricted and unconditional contributions;
• unrestricted and conditional contributions; and
• restricted and conditional contributions.

The type of contribution a particular transaction falls into depends on whether or not the donor has attached to it any conditions, restrictions or a combination of the two. Only the donor may place restrictions and conditions on a given contribution.

Knowing what type of contribution you have and accounting for it properly can potentially have major implications on the presentation of and interpretation of your press's financial statements. The primary difference between conditions and restrictions is that a condition specifies what the recipient (your press) must do or what must happen for it to receive the contribution, while a restriction specifies how and when the recipient can spend the contribution after it is received. Let's look at these differences more closely:

- **Conditions** deal with events (a future event or an uncertain event) which must occur before your press is entitled to *receive* (in the case of pledged funds) or *use* a contribution. Contributions received subject to conditions are not recorded as revenue by your press until the condition has been met. A contribution received with no conditions attached (unconditional contributions), however, is recorded as a contribution under nonoperating revenue upon receipt of the pledge or check, whichever comes first.

- **Restrictions** limit how your press can use a contribution after receiving it. Restrictions can be temporary or permanent.

The examples on page 58 should help simplify our explanation.

Reporting Conditional Contributions

Logic would tell us that most presses would not accept a pledge for a conditional contribution if they had no intention of meeting the donor's condition. Thus, it would seem that conditional pledges would be posted to the grants and contributions receivable account upon the press's acceptance of the pledge. From the perspective of the for-profit business world, this would seem to make sense because it would increase the net-asset value of the nonprofit organization. But incentives and regulations are different in the nonprofit realm!

Under FASB 116, conditional contributions are not *required* to be accounted for on the books until the condition has been met. In fact, if you look back at FASB 116's definition of a contribution (page 56), you'll see that a pledge is not considered a contribution unless, or until, it is *unconditional*. Likewise, granting organizations (foundations, government or corporate donors) do not have to record pledges for conditional contributions under their "contributions payable" account until the recipient meets the condition. This is despite the fact that they bear an obligation to pay if the condition is fulfilled.

All this leads one to wonder "Why wouldn't a nonprofit press want to include conditional grants as part of their contributions receivable account?" The main reason is that the contributions receivable account raises the press's net asset value. And a large net asset balance may give prospective donors the impression that the press has all the money it needs and therefore lead them to donate their resources elsewhere.

Unrestricted and Unconditional Contribution

A foundation awards your press a $10,000 grant to assist in funding general operations in the current fiscal year. The press records the contribution in the unrestricted class of contributions, listed under nonoperating revenue on the statement of activities.

Restricted and Unconditional Contribution

A foundation awards your press a $10,000 grant, stipulating that the funds must be used for production expenses related to the press's fall frontlist. This temporary restriction will be satisfied when the press incurs the appropriate production costs.

To account for this, the contribution would originally be recorded in the temporarily restricted class of contributions, listed under nonoperating revenue on the statement of activities. As the press satisfies the restriction requirements, the amount of the related expenses is recorded in the appropriate expense accounts for the balance sheet. The press must also move the same amount from the temporarily restricted class of contributions to the unrestricted class; this is done by reclassifying it on the line item entitled "contributions released from restrictions."

Unrestricted and Conditional Contribution

An individual pledges to contribute $5,000 to the press for its general operations, but the contribution will only be made if the press publishes a specific book by a particular author. This conditional contribution is not recognized as income in the accounting records until the condition has been satisfied. Once the press has published that particular book, the condition is met and the contribution is accounted for as in the first example above.

Restricted and Conditional Contribution

A foundation awards your press a $5,000 grant for the purchase of new computer equipment; however, the foundation will only make the grant if the press raises an additional $10,000 in funds for the same purpose. This is called a matching or challenge grant. Once the press can prove to the foundation that it has raised at least $10,000 for the purchase of new computer equipment, the condition will be met and the $5,000 grant from the foundation can be recorded as a temporarily restricted contribution under nonoperating revenue. When the computer equipment is purchased, the accounting proceeds as in the second example above.

Besides hindering fund-raising efforts, the increased net asset value that results when a conditional contribution is posted before the condition is met may actually be misleading. As in the third example in the box on page 58, the condition may be one that increases the press's expenses to an extent that consumes the entire amount of the conditional contribution—if not more.

···

Accounting for Contributed Services

FASB 116 covers one other area worth highlighting. Like other nonprofits, nonprofit publishers often rely on contributed services to manage their press, and though important to the smooth operations of the press, the value of these services is not always reflected in the financial statements. FASB 116 outlines the circumstances under which your press needs to recognize contributed services in your financial statements. If either of the following criteria is present, your press must place a value on contributed services and record them as contributions in its financial statements:

- the services create or enhance nonfinancial assets; or

- the services require specialized skills, are provided by persons possessing those skills, *and* would typically have to be purchased if not provided by donation.

If you have a volunteer bookkeeper, receive donated warehouse space or have enlisted someone's pro bono services to write a customized software program, you need to account for the fair market value of these services on your income statement. An accountant can guide you in how to properly value these services.

···

Summary

Being a nonprofit organization means that your press is subject to financial accounting standards that are unique and specific to the nonprofit industry. FASB 117 provides standards on the format and information to be included in external financial statements your press must prepare. FASB 116 defines contributions and sets forth requirements for the external financial statement reporting of the various types of contributions your press may receive. By adhering to these standards your press is fulfilling many of the requirements outside funders look for when evaluating the financial condition of your press.

chapter 6
· · · · · · · · · · · · · · · · · · · ·

Presenting a Positive and True Picture for Outsiders
Audit, Tax and Grant Compliance

Chapter Highlights

▶ **The Audit**

▶ **Internal Controls**

▶ **Tax and Compliance Reporting Requirements**

▶ **Unrelated Business Income**

▶ **Reporting for Private Donations**

▶ **Grant Reporting**

Presenting a Positive and True Picture for Outsiders
Audit, Tax and Grant Compliance

Until now, we have focused primarily on the internal accounting procedures and preparation of financial statements. These two areas provide the base of financial information that internal decision makers, such as the board of directors and management, need for making sound decisions about the press's overall direction and day-to-day operations. Though these same financial statements are often presented to external audiences, such as funders, the reporting process doesn't end there. As a nonprofit, your press will also need to report on its financial condition in very specific ways for outside funding purposes and to maintain its tax-exempt status. This chapter deals with the external reports and compliance documents that keep your press *legal* and in *good standing* with all. Often the first step in these external reporting processes is the *audit*.

The Audit

Say the word "audit" and many people in nonprofits go into a state of dread second only to that of budget preparation time. If approached properly, however, an audit should not be dreadful at all, but in many respects helpful and educational.

Why does your press need an audit? First, it's important to note that the financial statements your press prepares on a monthly basis are, in accounting lingo, "internal financial statements." This means they are compiled either by your in-house staff or by a financial or accounting consultant with whom you've contracted. These statements are designed primarily for internal use by management and the board. When it comes to approving grant applications, however, most foundations, government agencies and banks require *audited* financial statements from their grantees to ensure that those applying for grants have a history of appropriate spending.

An audit verifies that your press's financial statements are credible and that they provide reliable information. Audits are always performed by an independent outside party, usually a certified public accountant (CPA), in accordance with generally accepted auditing standards.

Selecting an Audit Firm

The selection of a CPA to perform the audit and provide other professional financial and consulting services to your press is a major decision that should not be taken lightly. You might begin the process by developing a list of several CPA firms you know to be reputable and that *have experience providing auditing services to other nonprofit organizations*. Experience with other nonprofit arts groups should be tops on your selection criteria list. Once you've narrowed down your choices, ask the remaining contenders to submit proposals for the services requested. After you've received the proposals, set up interviews with the firms you believe will provide your press with the desired results. Be sure in the interview process to ask about their experience with nonprofits *similar in size to your press*, as well as how they will treat certain areas of concern to you. One of the most troublesome audit issues for small publishers is the *valuation of inventory*. Ask specific questions about how they might treat your nonselling backlist.

The cost of an audit will always be a major consideration. Keep in mind that you often get what you pay for; a low bid does not have to mean this is the one you choose. Though free, a "pro bono" audit can raise more red flags with funders than it's worth if the accountants performing the audit don't understand nonprofit or publishing-industry accounting. When considering an accounting firm, be sure to ask the following questions:

- Who will be responsible for overseeing and performing the audit?

- What is that person's experience in nonprofit and publishing-industry accounting?

- What is the likelihood of that person continuing to do the audit in subsequent years?

- Is the person willing and available to assist with questions or problems that may come up during the rest of the year when the audit is not in progress?

Staff continuity, another important factor, is often directly related to the size of the auditing firm. The smaller the firm, the more likely the same staff will be around year after year to audit your press. That's a plus for you. You have enough of your own staff to break in each year without bringing in a new auditor each year, too!

Once you've chosen a CPA firm that suits your press, ask for an *engagement letter* detailing the work they are agreeing to perform, the price of their services and any other items agreed upon, such as work you may need to complete before the audit can begin. You will need to sign this engagement letter before any work on the audit can commence.

The more prepared your press is for the audit, the less time the auditor will need to spend at your offices and the sooner you will receive the audited financial statements. Before the audit begins, the auditor should provide you with a list of the financial statements and records he or she will need for the audit. By preparing most, if not all, of these records and statements before the auditor arrives, the audit process is more likely to proceed smoothly. If the auditor has to do the bookkeeping work you were supposed to have done, you could end up paying more for the audit. Figure 6-1 below provides a list of items you're likely to need for the audit.

Figure 6-1
Audit Preparation
Checklist

Audit Preparation Checklist

Documents
- ❏ Minutes of committee and board of directors meetings
- ❏ Grant and contract proposals and award letters
- ❏ Lease agreements
- ❏ Contracts with authors and distributors
- ❏ Payroll-related forms and reports
- ❏ Insurance policies
- ❏ Loans and notes payable
- ❏ Invoices and any correspondence from your press's attorney(s)

Financial Records
- ❏ Bank statements and bank reconciliations for all cash and investment accounts
- ❏ Year-to-date general ledger
- ❏ Financial statements and trial balance for the end of the period being audited
- ❏ Ledgers, journals and registers
- ❏ Vendor invoices

Work Papers
For Operating Revenues and Inventory:
- ❏ Detailed listing of accounts receivable at year-end
- ❏ Schedule of allowance for doubtful accounts and allowance for sales returns, with an explanation of how these amounts were arrived at
- ❏ Detailed listing of finished-book inventory and books in process at year-end
- ❏ Schedule of allowance for obsolete inventory, with an explanation of how this amount was arrived at
- ❏ Schedule of subsidiary rights income for the year
- ❏ Detailed year-end listing of royalty advances
- ❏ Depreciation schedule

Work Papers—*continued*
For Liabilities, Including Salaries:
- ❏ Detailed listing of accounts payable at year-end
- ❏ Detailed listing of any loans and notes payable at year-end, with computations for any accrued interest and a schedule of future loan payments
- ❏ Schedule of salaries payable at year-end
- ❏ Schedule of payroll taxes and employee benefits payable at year-end
- ❏ Schedule of year-to-date salaries and payroll taxes
- ❏ Detailed schedule of employee vacation earned but not used as of year-end
- ❏ Schedule of temporarily restricted contributions at year-end (in the past, this might have been considered deferred revenue)

For General Expenses:
- ❏ Schedule of professional fees (i.e., amounts paid to attorneys, accountants and consultants)
- ❏ Schedule of rent expense for the year
- ❏ Listing of supplies and equipment costing more than $300

For Contributions:
- ❏ Detailed listing of grants and contributions receivable
- ❏ Recap of in-kind contributions received during the year

Miscellaneous:
- ❏ Other schedules as requested by your auditor:

  _____

  _____

Getting a Clean Bill of Health

Among the various procedures the auditor is required to perform are the following two tests:

- *confirmation of accounts receivable* from outside parties; and
- observation of a *physical count of items held in inventory.*

Confirmation of receivables involves writing to those organizations, such as distributors, that owe your press large amounts of money and asking them to verify the amount owed, as shown on the press's books. Observation of a count of inventories involves the auditor going to each place where a substantial amount of books are stored and personally verifying the existence of the items shown as being held. Because the assets of most small nonprofit presses consist of large amounts of both accounts receivable and inventory, the successful completion of both of these tests is essential to the outcome of the audit.

Once the audit is completed, the auditor will issue an opinion on the "fairness" of your press's financial statements. Your objective is to receive an *unqualified* (or clean) opinion that attests to the credibility and reliability of your financial statements.

If the auditor was unable to obtain audit evidence about a matter that might materially affect the financial statements, he or she will issue a *qualified* opinion. An *adverse* opinion results when the financial statements and supporting documentation do not conform with generally accepted accounting principles. An adverse opinion is considered more severe than a qualified opinion because of the significance of the departure from generally accepted accounting principles. A *disclaimer of an opinion* results when the auditor is unable to form an opinion on the financial statements. If a disclaimer of opinion is issued, the reason for it is spelled out in the audit report. A qualified opinion, adverse opinion or disclaimer of an opinion reflects poorly on your press and sends a negative message to outside reviewers.

The following are among the financial statements for which the auditor will provide an opinion:

- the balance sheet;
- statement of activities;
- statement of changes in cash flows, which provides an historical perspective of the sources and uses of your press's cash for the period reported (not to be confused with the internal *cash-flow projection* discussed in Chapter 8);
- notes to the financial statements, which provide detailed information to support the numbers in the financial statements; and
- statement of functional expenses (not required, but strongly recommended).

Management Letter

In addition to the audit report, your board of directors should request a *management letter* from the auditor about the press's internal operations. The management letter lists any inadequacies in your press's accounting processes and recommends possible corrective actions. A management letter can be an extremely important source of information for both board members and management of a nonprofit organization.

....

Internal Controls

The extent of detailed testing the auditor will perform on your press's financial records is in large part dependent on the adequacy of the press's *internal controls* system. A strong system of internal controls means the auditor can rely more greatly on the press's internal financial information and thus perform fewer detailed or substantive tests. Auditors are trained to detect weaknesses in internal controls systems and are responsible for reporting such weaknesses to the press's management and board (usually through the management letter). Responsibility for ensuring that a strong system of internal controls is established and maintained, however, lies with your press's management and board of directors, not with the auditor.

What is an internal controls system and why, aside from the audit, should you be concerned about it? An internal controls system is a set of record-keeping, financial accounting and other procedures designed to safeguard an organization's assets and ensure the reliability of its financial records. A strong internal controls system improves the quality of financial information available and reduces the possibility that *error, mismanagement* or *fraud* will occur.

The cornerstone of any internal controls system is *segregation of duties*. This involves assigning responsibilities to personnel in such a manner that no one individual controls all aspects of a financial transaction. Segregation is a coordinated system of checks and balances to increase the likelihood of detecting errors, mismanagement or fraud, should they occur. Because of small staff size, many small nonprofit presses may not be able to incorporate all facets of strong internal controls into their operations. At a minimum, however, your press's leadership must be aware of and understand the elements needed to create a strong internal controls system and then do the best they can to implement as many as possible given the press's staff size. Consult with your CPA to design and implement an internal controls system appropriate for your press.

The best way to analyze the strength of your press's internal controls system is by asking the right questions. The checklist on the following pages should give you a good sense of where you stand on the question of internal controls. Don't be alarmed if your press does not have all the controls procedures listed. This is an opportunity to make a course correction to your current procedures.

Figure 6-2

Evaluating Your
Press's Internal
Controls System

Evaluating Your Press's Internal Controls System

Cash Receipts (✓)

- Cash receiving, processing, recording and bank reconciliation functions are clearly segregated. _____
- Checks received are listed individually on a control sheet for comparison with the bank deposit ticket. _____
- Checks are restrictively endorsed (stamped "for deposit only") by the person opening the mail. _____
- Cash is deposited intact (without any "temporary" withdrawals, say for petty cash purposes) in a bank account and on a timely basis. _____
- Duplicate deposit slips are prepared. _____
- Validated deposit slips are received from the bank and attached to the deposit detail. _____

Cash Disbursements

- Authorization, processing, check signing, recording and bank reconciliation functions are clearly segregated. _____
- Persons authorized to approve expenditures are clearly identified. _____
- Expenditures are approved in advance by authorized persons (such as through a purchase order system). _____
- Invoices or requests for expenditures are supported by appropriate documentation and approval(s). _____
- Supporting documents are canceled (i.e., stamped PAID) to prevent subsequent use. _____
- All cash disbursements are made by prenumbered checks. _____
- The person processing checks keeps a record of cash disbursements. _____
- Two signatures are required on each check or on all checks over a certain dollar amount. _____
- Signed checks are mailed promptly. _____
- Checks are controlled and accounted for with safeguards for returned and voided checks. _____
- Blank checks are properly controlled and securely stored. _____
- Checks written to "cash" are prohibited. _____
- Signing checks in advance is prohibited. _____
- Bank accounts are reconciled monthly. _____

Payroll

- The personnel authorization, payroll approval and preparation, payroll check distribution, record-keeping and bank reconciliation functions are clearly segregated. _____
- Changes in employment (new hires and terminations), salaries, wage rates and payroll deductions are authorized by proper personnel. _____
- Policies and procedures are in place for accounting for vacations, holidays and sick leave. _____
- Changes in employment status are recorded in employee personnel files. _____
- Time sheets for each employee are maintained and authorized by proper personnel. _____

Figure 6-2
Evaluating Your
Press's Internal
Controls System
(continued)

Payroll—*continued*   (✓)

- Payroll checks are always prepared after receipt of approved time sheets and based on those reports. _____
- All disbursements are made by prenumbered checks. _____
- The summary of the payroll register is posted to the general ledger on a timely basis. _____

Accounts Receivable

- Authorized prices for books are clearly established and effectively communicated to those responsible for the billing function. _____
- Changes in prices are promptly communicated. _____
- Billing is done by serially prenumbered invoices. _____
- The subsidiary receivables ledger is periodically balanced with general ledger control accounts. _____
- Follow-up action is taken on overdue balances. _____
- Collections are promptly recorded in receivables records. _____
- Outstanding accounts are properly analyzed for collectability and periodically aged. _____
- The write-off of uncollectable accounts is authorized by proper personnel. _____

Accounts Payable

- Authorization, processing, recording and payment functions are clearly segregated. _____
- All approved invoices are promptly recorded in the accounts payable register to establish control for payment. _____
- Unpaid invoices are maintained in a distinct unpaid invoice file. _____
- Statements from vendors are regularly compared with open invoice files. _____
- Invoices from unfamiliar or unusual vendors are reviewed and approved for payment by authorized personnel who are independent of the invoice processing function. _____
- Payments are promptly recorded in the accounts payable register to avoid double payment. _____
- The accounts payable register is periodically reconciled with the general ledger by a person independent of the invoice processing function. _____
- The organization obtains competitive bids for items whose cost exceeds a specified dollar amount. _____

Inventory

- Inventory purchasing, custodial, processing and record-keeping functions are clearly segregated. _____
- Responsibility for inventory is established and appropriate safeguards are maintained. _____
- The receipt, transfer and withdrawal of inventory items are promptly recorded in the inventory records and quantity records of inventory items are maintained. _____
- Inventory records are periodically reconciled with the general ledger. _____
- A physical inventory is periodically taken by persons independent of custody and processing functions. _____

Figure 6-2
Evaluating Your
Press's Internal
Controls System
(continued)

Fixed Assets (✓)

- Authorization, purchasing, custody and record-keeping functions are clearly segregated. _____
- Fixed asset purchases are permitted only if preapproved by the board. _____
- Borrowing for fixed asset purchases is limited to specific authorization by the board. _____
- The press has established policies covering capitalization and depreciation. _____
- Detailed records are maintained showing the asset values of individual units of property and equipment. _____
- Detailed property and equipment records are periodically balanced to the general ledger. _____
- Fixed assets are periodically appraised by an independent appraiser for insurance purposes. _____
- Detailed fixed asset records are periodically checked by physical inventory. _____
- Adequate procedures exist for the receiving and recording of gifts of fixed assets. _____
- Procedures exist governing the disposition of fixed assets. _____

Other

- Bank reconciliations are prepared as soon as possible after the bank statement is received. _____
- Bank statements are reconciled by someone other than the person(s) handling the cash receipt and cash disbursement functions. _____
- Financial statements are prepared on a timely, regular (monthly) basis and presented to appropriate board members, management and staff for review and discussion. _____
- The financial statements format allows for comparison of actual financial activity to budgeted amounts (variance analysis). _____
- The press has a fidelity insurance policy. _____
- Employee loans are prohibited. _____
- Investments are properly recorded and controlled. _____
- Contracts with authors are properly recorded and filed. _____
- Procedures are in place to document the receipt of in-kind services. _____
- Minutes from board of directors meetings are prepared on a timely basis. _____
- Insurance policies are reviewed annually and provide adequate coverage. _____

Tax and Compliance Reporting Requirements

Even though your press has been granted tax-exempt status as a 501(c)(3) organization, it still must file annual returns to the Internal Revenue Service and to the state in which it does business. Because the tax and compliance area can be very technical and correspondent regulations and reporting requirements change constantly, we strongly recommend that you consult with competent legal and accounting advisors to ensure that you are complying with all applicable federal and state reporting requirements and procedures.

Annual Information Return Form 990

As long as your press continues to operate according to the premises by which it obtained its 501(c)(3) tax-exempt status, it does not have to pay income taxes. In lieu of preparing and filing an annual income tax return, as commercial enterprises are required to do, your nonprofit press must instead file an annual information return with the IRS. The form used for this purpose is *Form 990: Return of Organization Exempt From Income Tax.*

Form 990 must be filed by the 15th day of the fifth month after the end of your fiscal year. So, if your press operates on a calendar-year basis, the informational return is due May 15. If your fiscal year ends on June 30, the due date is November 15. Failure to file the return on time will result in a penalty. Extensions of time for filing can usually be obtained if there is good reason why the return could not be filed by the deadline; but the application for extension must be made before the original filing deadline.

Form 990 may be prepared internally, but most nonprofits contract with a CPA firm (usually the same firm that does their audit) to prepare all federal and state tax reporting and compliance forms. This is money well spent! We highly recommend that you have your CPA include preparation of all tax and compliance reports as one of the services provided under the audit engagement letter.

Once filed, your press's Form 990 becomes a matter of public record. Except for the listing of contributors, the entire return and all attached statements and schedules are available for public inspection upon request through the IRS and, in most states, through the state attorney general's office. Your press is also obligated to make it available to anyone who asks. These requirements all speak to the fact that tax-exempt nonprofits receive public support and because of this, are subject to greater accountability to the public than are their commercial counterparts.

Proper preparation and timely filing of Form 990 is essential to maintaining your press's good standing with the IRS and its 501(c)(3) tax-exempt status.

....

State Compliance Requirements

In addition to federal filing and reporting requirements, most states require nonprofit organizations to register with and submit financial reports to one or more state agencies. Most states require nonprofits to register with a state regulatory agency before soliciting funds from within the state. This registration often requires yearly renewals, as well as filing of an annual financial report. Many states will accept a copy of IRS Form 990 as the basic financial statement, while others require an audited financial statement in addition to the 990. In most states, these annual reports are due sometime between three and six months after the end of each organization's fiscal year.

Because reporting requirements vary from state to state, we encourage you to consult with competent legal or tax advisors who are familiar with the laws and requirements for nonprofit organizations in the state in which you do business.

....

Unrelated Business Income

If your press engages in activities that generate *unrelated business income*, it may be required to pay *unrelated-business income tax* (UBIT). For example, if your press purchased a building to house its own operations as well as to rent at commercial rates to nonpublishing professionals or businesses, the rent it receives from commercial tenants may be taxable as unrelated-business income.

The IRS has three criteria for unrelated trade or business activity:

- the activity is not substantially related to the purpose for which the nonprofit received tax-exempt status;
- the activity must be a trade or business; and
- the activity must be regularly carried on.

All three of these criteria must be present for an activity to be categorized as an unrelated trade or business activity. If the three criteria are present, your press is subject to UBIT on the net income generated by this activity (revenues minus the costs normally associated with the unrelated activity).

To report on and to determine the amount of unrelated-business income and tax liability, the IRS requires all nonprofits engaged in such activities to file Form 990-T, which is an attachment to Form 990. Because this is a highly complex area of the tax law, we strongly recommend that you consult with a competent tax advisor to determine any potential tax implications your press might face before it embarks on other business activities.

....

Reporting for Private Donations

If a donor contributes $250 or more in cash or property to your press during a given year, you must provide written acknowledgment to the donor to substantiate the donor's charitable tax deduction. A canceled check is not sufficient in this case. Your press should be prepared to assist its individual and corporate donors with substantiation of their contributions.

Whenever a donor receives something of value in return for a charitable contribution, only the amount of the contribution that is in excess of the fair market value of the goods or services received may be deducted as a charitable contribution on the donor's income tax return. If the total amount received is greater than $75, the nonprofit organization must inform the donor in clearly stated language what portion of the contribution, if anything, is deductible.

For example, say your press sponsors a special fund-raising event that includes a dinner. A comparable dinner in a restaurant would cost the donor $25, but your donors are paying $100 each to attend the fund-raising dinner. In this case, your press would be responsible for informing each donor that only $75 of their $100 payment is deductible as a charitable deduction.

If your press fails to comply with the notification requirements described above, the IRS may impose penalties.

....

Grant Reporting

For most grants and contracts received from foundations, and sometimes individuals, your press will be required to submit financial reports detailing what the press accomplished with the use of the funds and how and where the money was spent. Depending on the grantor's guidelines, such reporting may be required periodically throughout a designated project or program, at the end of the project, or both.

If your accounting system has been set up to account for specific contributions, especially those with restrictions, the preparation of the requested financial reports should be relatively easy. If, however, your press's accounting system lacks the capability of tracking expenses related to a specific contribution, or if spreadsheets detailing these expenses have not been prepared, a lot more work will have to be done to prepare these reports. By tracking expenses related to specific grants through an ongoing accounting process, your press helps ensure that the financial information presented to grantors is accurate and supported by proper documentation.

Just as important as the accuracy of these reports is submitting them on a timely basis. Whenever your press receives a grant, it is imperative that the award letter be scrutinized for reporting requirements and the due dates of required reports. The due dates of each of the required reports should then be entered chronologically into some type of tickler system, with reminders set far enough in advance of the due date(s) to allow adequate time for each report to be carefully completed and submitted.

Grant reporting should not be thought of as just something that "has to be done." A substantial amount of the money that it takes to support your press's programs comes from contributed sources. In today's economic climate, many nonprofit presses are finding it increasingly difficult to obtain grants. The thought and effort you put into preparing grant reports may help improve the chance of your press receiving another grant from that donor, especially if the reports show that the money received was used responsibly and for its intended purpose.

Summary

It is not enough for your press just to prepare a set of financial statements on a regular basis. The financial statements and any information that supports them needs to be communicated to the board of directors, funders and creditors.

Besides the internal financial statements prepared by your press on a regular basis, it must also prepare (usually annually) more formal financial reports such as an audit and an IRS Form 990. Audited financial statements alert the reader that an independent third party (a CPA) has performed specific tests on the press's financial transactions that allow the CPA to form an opinion as to the credibility and reliability of the information presented in the financial statements. Your press's goal is to obtain a clean bill of health—or an *unqualified* opinion—from the CPA on its financial statements.

The audit process is quite involved and there are certain things your press should do to ensure it goes as smoothly as possible. The first is to select an auditor that is familiar with the nonprofit industry (preferably the nonprofit press industry). It is also important to choose someone who will provide you with professional services not just during the audit, but on an as-needed basis throughout the year. Two other factors that can help the audit process proceed smoothly are a strong system of internal controls and compiling as much information as possible before the auditor arrives to begin the fieldwork.

Other financial reports required for the press to maintain its nonprofit, tax-exempt status and its ability to receive contributions include IRS Form 990, reports required by the state in which your press is incorporated and grant reports to foundations or corporations that have contributed money to support the programs of the press.

chapter 7
·······················

Publishing Pitfalls
Accounting for Inventory, Royalties and Returns

Chapter Highlights

▶ **Book Inventory**

▶ **Inventory Costs**

▶ **The Relationship Between Inventory and Cost of Books Sold**

▶ **Recognizing Gross Profit From Book Sales**

▶ **Royalty Expense**

▶ **Book Returns**

▶ **Distribution**

Publishing Pitfalls
Accounting for Inventory, Royalties and Returns

The accounting issues you face as a small nonprofit press are in many ways more complex than those of other nonprofit organizations or your commercial counterparts. Because you publish books as a tax-exempt organization, you must find an effective way to account for both your production costs *and* book sales and the contributions your press receives.

With the new FASB requirements, the accounting profession has provided increased guidance on how to account for contributions and report to external funders. But helpful as they may be, these standards don't address many of the accounting concerns unique to the small nonprofit publisher.

Currently, wide inconsistencies exist in the way small nonprofit presses (and their auditors) account for items like book inventory and cost of books sold. Within the industry, inconsistent accounting treatment of fundamental publishing functions is problematic because it makes it very difficult, if not impossible, to compare the financial condition of one press with that of another. It also hinders the industry as a whole, as well as individual presses, when attempting to legitimize the industry and its accounting practices in the eyes of outside funders.

This chapter tackles the more technical accounting issues associated with nonprofit publishing, including:

- accounting for book inventory;
- inventory obsolescence;
- the relationship between inventory and cost of books sold;
- calculating royalty expenses; and
- accounting for book returns and distribution.

Throughout the chapter, we will offer specific recommendations for the field. If any of these topics are of interest to you, read on—or, better yet, give it to your auditor to read.

Book Inventory

Book inventory is an asset consisting of books in process of being completed and books that are finished and being held for future sale. For most small nonprofit presses, book inventory makes up a significant portion of the press's current assets and, quite probably, of its total assets. Accounting for book inventory is one of the most complex record-keeping procedures your press must perform. Three major factors contribute to this complexity. First, your press must have a mechanism in place to track how many books it has in its inventory at any given time. Second, it must know the value of these books. And third, the press's leadership must be aware of the correlation between book inventory on the balance sheet and cost of books sold on the statement of activities.

Accounting for the actual quantities of books in your press's inventory may be done in one of two ways: by a *periodic (physical) inventory system* or a *perpetual inventory system*. The major differences between these two methods is that the perpetual inventory system uses detailed subsidiary ledgers in the perpetual book inventory register (see Chapter 3) for each title in your press's inventory. These ledgers tell you on an ongoing basis:

- the number of copies on hand at the beginning of the accounting period;
- the number of copies currently on hand;
- the number of copies sold;
- the dollar value of the inventory; and
- the amount of money currently invested in books in process (as opposed to finished books).

In contrast, in the periodic inventory system, the only accounting performed is done at the end of a period, at which time the books in stock are physically counted and any adjustments between the beginning and ending inventory values are recorded. The perpetual inventory system provides major advantages over the periodic inventory system because it tells you exactly how many books are available at any given time and it helps safeguard your inventory from pilferage and other loss. For these reasons, we recommend that your press use a perpetual inventory system, even though it does require more record keeping than the periodic inventory system. Under the perpetual inventory system, you will still have to physically count your press's book inventory, but usually only once a year to verify the accuracy of your accounting records.

Accounting for Inventory-Related Transactions

Accounting for your press's book inventory involves posting for several interrelated transactions in several balance sheet and statement of activities accounts. To help clarify the flow of inventory-related transactions in the accounting system, let's look at a simplified example designed to encompass the whole process. Note that though your press's actual balance sheet will include two line items for inventory—"finished books" and "books in process"—we will use only one account entitled "book inventory." To simplify the example further, we will assume that your press started the year with a beginning inventory of zero. Use the "footnote" numbers that follow the descriptions of each transaction to help you see where each transaction was posted. Now, on to the example:

Example

During the first six months of the year, your press published 4,000 copies of one 250-page book. Total cost to produce this book, excluding royalty expenses, was $15,000[1] (or a per-unit cost of $3.75), which the press paid promptly the day after receipt of the bill on June 3.[2] Beginning of the year cash balance was $20,000. The entries to record these costs and subsequent payments in your accounting system include:

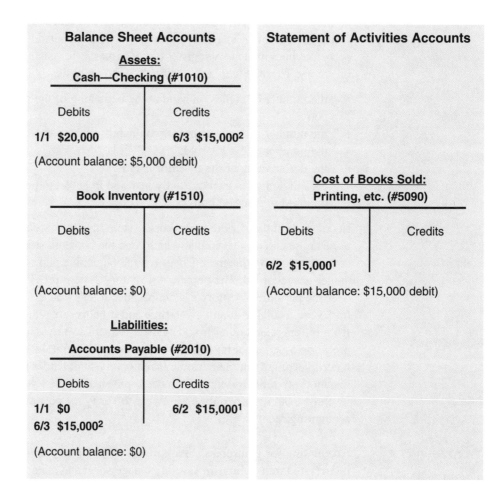

| **Balance Sheet Accounts** | | **Statement of Activities Accounts** |

Assets:
Cash—Checking (#1010)

Debits	Credits
1/1 $20,000	6/3 $15,000[2]

(Account balance: $5,000 debit)

Book Inventory (#1510)

Debits	Credits

(Account balance: $0)

Cost of Books Sold:
Printing, etc. (#5090)

Debits	Credits
6/2 $15,000[1]	

(Account balance: $15,000 debit)

Liabilities:
Accounts Payable (#2010)

Debits	Credits
1/1 $0	6/2 $15,000[1]
6/3 $15,000[2]	

(Account balance: $0)

No entry is made to the inventory account on the balance sheet at this time, but all of the information is recorded in the perpetual book inventory register for transfer later to the balance sheet.

Perpetual Book Inventory Register

Date	Description	Book #	# of Copies	Debit	Credit
1/1	Beginning inventory		0	$ 0	
6/2	Printing, etc for "Title A"[1]	#001	4,000	$15,000	

Now at the end of the fiscal year in December, your press and the distributor have sold (net of returns) 1,500 copies at $12.95 each (not including discounts) for a total sales income of $19,425.[3] To date, your press has received $12,500[4] of this amount in cash. To account for these sales and cash receipts you would record the following entries:

Balance Sheet Accounts
Assets:
Cash—Checking (#1010)

Debits	Credits
1/1 $20,000	6/3 $15,000[2]
12/31 $12,500[4]	

(Account balance: $17,500 debit)

Accounts Receivable (#1210)

Debits	Credits
12/31 $19,425[3]	12/31 $12,500[4]

(Account balance: $6,925 debit)

Statement of Activities

Book Sales (#40XX)

Debits	Credits
	12/31 $19,425[3]

(Account balance $19,425 credit)

You might think the accounting process is finished at this point, but the most important procedure in this inventory accounting process has not yet been performed. An adjustment has to be made to properly state the book inventory account on the balance sheet and to properly state cost of books sold on the statement of activities. The procedures for doing this begin in the perpetual book inventory register.

You know that book inventory at the beginning of the year was zero; you added 4,000 copies of a book that cost a total of $15,000 to produce; you then sold 1,500 copies of the book which, at a cost of $3.75 per book, gives you a total cost of books sold of $5,625.[5] Your ending inventory now includes 2,500 books at a per book cost of $3.75 or a total dollar value of $9,375.[6] The accounting entries to account for this are as follows:

Perpetual Book Inventory Register

Date	Description	Book #	# of Copies	Debit	Credit
1/1	Beginning inventory		0	$ 0	
6/2	Printing, etc for "Title A"[1]	#001	4,000	$15,000	
12/31	Books removed for sales, distributor and direct[5]	#001	(1500)		$5,625
12/31	**Ending Inventory[6]**		**2,500**	**$ 9,375**	

Balance Sheet Accounts	Statement of Activities Accounts
	Cost of Books Sold:
Book Inventory (#1510)	**Printing, etc. (#5090)**
Debits / Credits	Debits / Credits
12/31 $9,375[6]	6/2 $15,000[1] / 12/31 $9,375[6]
(Account balance: $9,375 debit)	(Account balance: $5,625 debit)

Book sales:	$19,425
Less COBS:	($ 5,625)
Profit from sales:	$13,800

Inventory Costs

Because book inventory normally constitutes the single largest asset on the balance sheet of a small nonprofit press, tracking and verifying the inventory value is very important. Most small nonprofit presses have two primary questions or concerns when it comes to accounting for their book inventory:

- What costs are or should be included in book inventory?
- At what point, if at all, should a book be considered obsolete and no longer as part of the inventory value of your press (inventory obsolescence)?

**Determining
Inventory Value**

As explained in earlier chapters, your press should be accounting for all of its financial activity on the accrual basis. With that in mind, any costs incurred to produce a book should not be recorded as an expense, but rather as a part of book inventory. Accountants call this process capitalizing costs and the accumulation of all of these costs represents a capital investment in inventory.

All of the separate inventory costs for a particular book are aggregated to come up with a total inventory value for that book. Then, to arrive at a unit cost, the total inventory value for the book cost is divided by the number of copies printed. The book retains this value until it is sold, given away, discarded or lost. This process of tracking book costs to arrive at a total inventory value is pretty straightforward. What's not so straightforward is determining what costs should be included in book inventory.

Most for-profit businesses that have inventory as part of their operations must account for their inventory subject to specific IRS rules and regulations. Because your small nonprofit press is not subject to income tax on profits from book sales, you are allowed some flexibility in accounting for your press's book inventory. Before implementing any of the following suggestions and procedures, we strongly recommend that you consult with a competent tax advisor as to the tax implications, if any, of how your press accounts for the value of its inventory.

With the exception of costs associated with the editorial function and salary expenses, any cost that can be directly attributed to the production of a specific book should be considered an inventory cost. Costs considered to be a part of book inventory include, but are not limited to:

- paper, printing and binding;
- manuscript acquisition fees;
- permission fees;
- rights payments;
- translation fees;
- services performed by outside consultants or vendors, including cover design, artwork, copyediting, proofreading and typesetting; and
- any shipping costs associated with the manufacturing process (for example, the cost to move the books from the bindery to the warehouse).

Although salaries for in-house editorial staff are a necessary cost of producing books, accurately allocating these costs to individual books could be a very difficult and time-consuming task. For example, an editor reads many manuscripts before deciding which one(s) will ultimately be published. But to which published book would you allocate this cost and how would you determine the appropriate amount to charge? Would the total expense be assigned to the one book that gets published? Rather than worrying about such details, it's far easier to code these costs as *expenses of the editorial function*.

Other expenses *excluded* from the book inventory value include:

- postage;
- shipping and courier charges;
- supplies;
- telephone expenses;
- author royalty fees; and
- distribution fees.

Distribution and royalty expenses are not inventoriable costs, but they are considered to be an expense under cost of books sold. Both of these items will be discussed in-depth later.

Inventory Obsolescence

Unfortunately there is no industry standard for determining the obsolescence of a book. Small presses that do make an effort to account for book obsolescence are doing so using their best judgment. The IRS, supported by a Supreme Court decision, stipulates that it is illegal for *taxpaying* organizations to "write down" an inventory's value until the entity has actually lost the money. In the case of a for-profit publisher, money would be considered lost when the books were sold for less than their inventory cost or they were destroyed or discarded.

As a tax-exempt publisher, your press is allowed some flexibility when considering whether or not to set up a reserve for obsolete or slow-moving inventory. To create some consistency in this practice among small nonprofit presses, we recommend the process described below.

Recommended Process for Determining Obsolescence

At the end of every fiscal year, the sales history of all titles in the press's inventory should be reviewed. If sales of a particular title in the current year are less than sales of that title in any of the prior three years, the book may be considered to have a diminished market value. It is then up to the management—preferably in consultation with the press's auditor—to decide if that book's market value (sales potential) is less than the actual cost of the book. If it is, an accounting adjustment to reflect a more realistic market value may be in order. In accounting terms, this is called the "lower of cost or market" basis of accounting for inventory.

Rather than actually writing off the inventory value for each title with a market value less than its cost, the accounting adjustment is made to an account entitled "reserve for inventory obsolescence" (a credit) on the balance sheet and to an account entitled "obsolete inventory adjustment" (a debit) in the cost of books sold section of the statement of activities. The *reserve for inventory obsolescence* account is a contra-asset account (with a credit balance) on the balance sheet; when combined with the inventory account, the result is the *net book inventory value.*

At the end of each fiscal year, analyze your press's book inventory and compile an amount for obsolete inventory based on the above procedures. The reserve for obsolete inventory account on the balance sheet should then be adjusted accordingly. Remember, the procedures used for determining book obsolescence are based on your judgment and if performed, must be consistently applied on a year-to-year basis. Also, any procedures performed and adjustments made should be thoroughly documented.

Example

Reporting Inventory Obsolescence

At the end of the fiscal year, your press has 1,000 copies (out of a first printing of 4,500 copies) of Title A, valued at an original cost of $5 per copy, or $5,000. In the current fiscal year, your press sold only 100 copies of Title A. In the preceding three fiscal years Title A had sales of 2,000, 900 and 500 copies. Because sales in the current year were less than in any of the preceding three years, management decides that Title A's market value has been reduced and that this reduction should be reflected on the financial statements. Title A is considered to have no current market value. Your press would make the following accounting entries.

	Debit	Credit
Obsolete Inventory Adjustment	$5,000	
Reserve for Obsolete Inventory		$5,000

Assuming that the total value your press's book inventory is $75,000, the net inventory value is now $70,000 and is reflected on the balance sheet as follows:

	Debit	Credit
Inventory	$75,000	
Reserve for Obsolescence		$5,000

If these 1,000 copies of Title A were subsequently remaindered, the reserve for obsolescence account would be reduced (debited) to zero and only now would the actual inventory value also be reduced (credited).

	Debit	Credit
Reserve for Obsolete Inventory	$5,000	
Inventory		$5,000

The Relationship Between Inventory and Cost of Books Sold

The cost of every book you've published but not yet sold constitutes your *book inventory* and is accounted for as an asset on the balance sheet. Every time a book is sold, the unit cost of that book is subtracted from the *book inventory account* on the balance sheet and at the same time is added to the *cost of books sold account* on the statement of activities. The difference between the sales price received for the book and the unit cost of the book, plus associated distribution and royalty expenses, constitutes the profit you made on that particular book.

Figure 7-1 below illustrates both the proper way and an improper way to account for inventory and cost of goods sold. The proper way shows that there was $50,000 worth of book inventory at the beginning of the month. During the month, the press incurred paper, printing and binding costs of $20,000, which were added to inventory, and it sold books with a total inventory value of $5,000. Accordingly, inventory at the end of the month shows a $15,000 increase, bringing the value to $65,000.

The improper example indicates that the press recorded all of the paper, printing and binding costs as general operating expenses and made no adjustments to the inventory account to reflect these additional costs or to reduce inventory by the cost of the books sold. Following this way of accounting, the press's inventory value is understated by $15,000 and likewise its cost of books sold is overstated by $15,000.

If not accounted for properly during the year, your CPA will make adjustments during the audit to properly reflect the value of your press's inventory and cost of books sold. If you don't like surprises, however, don't wait for the annual audit. You owe it to your press's leadership to prepare and present monthly financial reports that contain accurate data derived from proper accounting methods.

Figure 7-1

Proper and Improper Ways for Calculating Inventory and Cost of Books Sold

Accounting for Inventory and Cost of Books Sold

		Proper Accounting	Improper Accounting
BALANCE SHEET			
Book Inventory—Beginning of Month		$ 50,000	$ 50,000
Plus: Costs Added to Inventory	(+)	20,000	
Less: Cost of Books Sold	(-)	5,000	
Book Inventory—End of Month	(=)	$ 65,000	$ 50,000
STATEMENT OF ACTIVITIES			
Beginning Inventory		$ 50,000	
Plus: Paper, Printing and Binding	(+)	20,000	$ 20,000
Cost of Books Available for Sale	(=)	70,000	
Less: Ending Inventory	(-)	65,000	
Subtotal—Cost of Books Sold	(=)	5,000	20,000
Plus: Distribution Expenses	(+)	5,000	5,000
Plus: Royalty Expense	(+)	3,000	3,000
Equals: Total Cost of Books Sold	(=)	$ 13,000	$ 28,000

Use the following formula to arrive at an amount for cost of books sold:

Calculating
Cost of Books Sold

Calculating Cost of Books Sold

	Beginning Inventory
Plus:	Costs Added to Inventory
Less:	Obsolete Inventory Adjustment
Equals:	Cost of Books Available for Sale
Less:	Ending Inventory
Equals:	Subtotal—Cost of Books Sold
Plus:	Distribution Expenses
Plus:	Royalty Expense
Equals:	Total Cost of Books Sold

Recognizing Gross Profit from Book Sales

Currently, many small press operations don't recognize *gross profit from book sales* on their statements of activities. We urge you to use a statement of activities format that allows you to easily identify *book sales*, *cost of books sold* and the *gross profit* from books sold.

The two statement of activities examples presented in Figure 7-2 (page 86) result in the same amount on the bottom line ($33,000) but use two different formats. Format A is how many small nonprofit presses currently present information on the results of their activities. It accounts for all the information necessary, but presents it in a way that is disjointed and not conducive to financial analysis.

On the other hand, by presenting *book sales, cost of books sold* and *gross profit from book sales* in a readily identifiable format, Format B is more conducive to further analysis and decision making. It allows for calculation of operating ratios and clearly establishes the amount of fund-raising support needed to subsidize your publishing efforts.

By placing cost of books sold directly below book sales, Format B also allows you to determine the press's gross operating profit. Because most small nonprofit presses have never presented these items in this fashion, no one really knows what an acceptable gross profit percentage is for their own press or for the small nonprofit industry as a whole. If all small nonprofit presses were to present financial information in this format, financial trend information could be compiled for the industry and used by management for comparison, analysis and decision-making purposes.

Remember, producing and selling books is a business and your small nonprofit press needs to use financial principles and analysis just like any commercial publisher would in analyzing the effectiveness and efficiency of it operations. We think you'll see the advantages of Format B and strongly urge you to adopt it.

Figure 7-2

Optional Statement
of Activities Formats

Optional Statement of Activities Formats

FORMAT A (Traditional)		FORMAT B (Preferred)	
Support and Revenue:		**Operating Revenue:**	
Support:		Book Sales—Net of Discounts	
Contributions (including in-kind		and Returns	$ 150,000
contributions of $10,000)	$ 185,000	Rights Revenue	5,000
Special Events—Net	5,000	**Total Operating Revenue**	**155,000**
Total Support	190,000		
		Cost of Books Sold	**(90,000)**
		Gross Profit Margin	**65,000**
Revenue:		**Other Operating Revenue**	**3,000**
Book Revenue—Net of			
Returns	150,000	**Operating Expenses**	**(225,000)**
Rights Income	5,000		
Miscellaneous Revenue	3,000	**Surplus (Deficit) from**	
Total Revenue	158,000	**Operations**	**(157,000)**
Total Support and Revenue	**348,000**	**Nonoperating Revenue**	
		Contributions	175,000
Expenses		In-Kind Contributions	10,000
(includes cost of books sold)	**(315,000)**	Special Events	10,000
		Special Events Costs	(5,000)
Change in Net Assets	**$ 33,000**	Total Nonoperating	
		Revenue	190,000
		Change in Net Assets	**$ 33,000**

....

Royalty Expense

In nearly all cases, at the time a press agrees to publish a book, it enters into a *royalty agreement* with the book's author(s). A royalty agreement stipulates that an author will receive a specified rate (usually a percentage of the cover price) for every copy of his or her book sold by the press. It is customary for presses to pay the author an advance on future royalties even before the press begins to offer the book for sale. The amount of the advance varies from press to press and from author to author, with no rules or guidelines dictating what amount is most appropriate.

Accounting for authors' royalties requires that detailed records be kept of the press's book sales. Your press's accounting or spreadsheet system must be capable of tracking book sales by title and then applying the royalty rate to the dollar value of sales for that book. How often royalties are calculated and paid may be different for each press. At minimum, however, royalties should be calculated semi-annually, if not quarterly.

A somewhat tricky aspect of royalty calculations is accounting for advances. Until an author has actually *earned* a royalty based on sales of his or her book, any advance royalty payments should be recorded as a prepaid expense on the balance sheet. For example, let's say an author receives a $3,000[1] advance on a book with an initial print run of 4,000 copies, a retail price of $12.95 and a royalty rate of 7.5% of the cover price for all books sold. This means that, if all books are sold, the author could ultimately receive $3,885 in royalties (4,000 copies x $12.95 per book x 7.5%). The following entry would be made to record the advance:

Balance Sheet Accounts

Assets:

Cash—Checking (#1010)		Royalty Advance (#1410)	
Debits	Credits	Debits	Credits
1/1 $20,000		7/1 $3,000[1]	
	7/1 $3,000[1]		
(Account balance: $17,000 debit)		(Account balance: $3,000 debit)	

Royalty payment calculations on October 31 show that 3,500 copies of this particular book have been sold. The total royalty expense for this book is $3,400[2] (3,500 x $12.95 x 7.5%). You've already paid the author a $3,000 advance, so you only owe him or her $400, which you pay in November.[3] To account for these transactions you would use the entries noted at the top of page 88.

Remember that as more books are sold, you will owe the author additional royalties. If all of the books are sold, the amount owed would be $485 ($3,885 minus the $3,400 already paid). A key management concept to remember here is that you are only calculating royalty payments periodically (i.e., quarterly or semi-annually), so you need to ensure that your press has enough cash on hand to make these royalty payments when they become due. A good way to plan for these payments is to estimate, based on current sales information, how much these royalty payments might be and reserve cash to cover this amount. That way, when the actual royalty calculations are made, a significant portion of the amount due will have already been set aside.

Also, based on the previous discussions of inventory and cost of books sold, note that royalty expense, although not a direct cost of producing a book (i.e., an inventory cost), is included in the calculation of total cost of books sold.

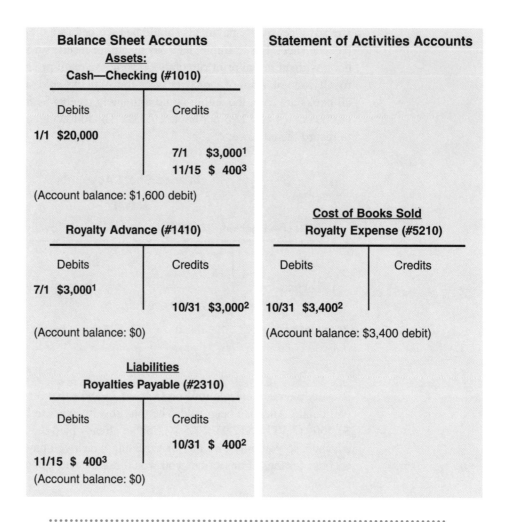

Balance Sheet Accounts
Assets:
Cash—Checking (#1010)

Debits	Credits
1/1 $20,000	
	7/1 $3,000[1]
	11/15 $ 400[3]

(Account balance: $1,600 debit)

Royalty Advance (#1410)

Debits	Credits
7/1 $3,000[1]	
	10/31 $3,000[2]

(Account balance: $0)

Liabilities
Royalties Payable (#2310)

Debits	Credits
	10/31 $ 400[2]
11/15 $ 400[3]	

(Account balance: $0)

Statement of Activities Accounts

Cost of Books Sold
Royalty Expense (#5210)

Debits	Credits
10/31 $3,400[2]	

(Account balance: $3,400 debit)

Book Returns

Returns of books that have already been sold are a fact of life in the publishing industry, especially for those presses that have contracted with a distributor to provide warehouse and book-distribution services. Sales returns are difficult to plan for, and if significant, have the potential of severely affecting the financial management of any press. Accordingly, you need to be keenly aware of the role sales returns play in the current economic climate of the publishing industry and ensure that procedures are in place to minimize their impact on your press.

As best you can, review previous and current years' sales returns to determine the overall average return rate (a percentage of total distributor sales) your press has experienced during the time frame used. Once this sales return rate has been determined, use it in the budget process, when preparing cash-flow projections and with the day-to-day accounting of your press's financial activities.

For example, say that on average 20 percent of all sales made by your distributor are returned. When you receive your monthly sales report from the distributor, it indicates sales of $50,000[1] for your press that month, which you record in the balance sheet accounts receivable account and in the statement of activities' sales account. But you know from experience that your press may only receive $40,000 ($50,000 X 20 percent). To record this, you need to make a $10,000[2] entry (credit) to an account entitled *allowance for sales returns* on the balance sheet and an entry for the same amount (debit) to an account entitled *sales returns* on the statement of activities as follows:

Balance Sheet Accounts		Statement of Activities Accounts	
Assets:			
Accounts Receivable (#1210)		**Distributor Sales (#4020)**	
Debits	Credits	Debits	Credits
8/3 $50,000[1]			8/3 $50,000[1]
(Account balance: $50,000 debit)		(Account balance: $50,000 credit)	
Allowance for Sales Returns (#1410)		**Sales Returns (#4120)**	
Debits	Credits	Debits	Credits
	8/3 $10,000[2]	8/3 $10,000[2]	
(Account balance: $10,000 credit)		(Account balance: $10,000 debit)	

Once you've established an "allowance for sales returns" account, you will want to maintain a balance representing 20 percent of total accounts receivable from your distributor, unless a significant change in the rate of returns transpires. Accounting for returns can be very complex and confusing. Consult a CPA (perhaps your press's auditor) if you would like more technical advice on applying this concept to your press's accounting practices.

....

Distribution

Most small presses contract with a distributor to provide representation, sales, billing, shipping, customer service, collections and processing of returns. These types of agreements vary from press to press and from distributor to distributor; however, most distributors charge publishers they represent a *percentage of sales net of returns* for these services. Furthermore, in most cases, your distributor will not send you the total amount of the monthly sale, but rather spread the payment of these receivables over three or four months to allow the distributor time to collect from the retailers that ordered your press's books.

On a monthly basis though, the distributor will usually compile a report detailing and recapping that month's sales, returns, the distribution fee, accounts receivable due the press and a timeline indicating when payment on these receivables can be expected. From these reports, your press must then prepare journal entries to account for all of the information contained in the report.

One last thing to remember: The distributor's fee is not included in the press's inventory value of any particular books, but should be considered in the calculation of *total cost of books sold*.

chapter 8

Concentrating on Cash

Chapter Highlights

▶ **Forecasting Cash Flow**

▶ **Borrowing Money**

Concentrating on Cash

Forecasting Cash Flow

Does this situation sound familiar? Your press has produced several new books, for which a large portion of expenses are currently due. Meanwhile, your distributor owes you a substantial amount of money for a recent exceptionally good sales month. Or you know that the press will be receiving a $50,000 grant from a major foundation, but these funds will not be received for two months; meanwhile, you have outstanding operating expenses, payroll due at the end of the week and not enough cash on hand. These are the classic cash-flow problems of a small nonprofit press.

Because a significant portion of your press's resources are tied up in inventory and accounts receivable, cash—or the lack of it—will be your constant concern. You need to figure out a way to determine if your press will have enough cash on hand when needed to meet operating expenses. How will you know this? Through *cash-flow forecasting*, or *projections*.

The cash-flow projection is an internal report that displays cash you expect to receive, the cash you expect to disburse, the difference between the two and the resulting projected cash balance. This report requires careful thought to prepare and should not be taken lightly.

If properly and regularly prepared, the cash-flow projection can help your press identify potential *negative cash-flow situations*, sometimes months in advance. This early warning may enable you to take steps to avert a crisis.

A key point to note here is that negative cash flow occurs when the demand for cash is higher than the cash currently on hand. Negative cash flow assumes that within the course of the year there will be enough money to handle financial obligations—it just isn't here now. Sometimes negative cash flow can look a lot like a *deficit,* but they are not the same thing. A *deficit* occurs when a press overspends its income on an annual basis. Negative cash flow, on the other hand, is a *temporary* situation, a timing problem with the receipt of cash.

Like any problem, the more advance warning you have of an impending negative cash-flow situation, the more options you will likely have at your disposal. Such options might include:

- setting up payment plans with your vendors;
- cutting back on other operating expenses;
- talking with your press's distributor or one of its grantors to see if the press can receive an advance payment on funds due it; or
- talking to a bank or other lender about the possibility of a short-term or working-capital loan.

Figure 8-1 (page 94) shows a cash-flow projection format for a typical nonprofit press. The projection begins with a listing of all sources of income (receipts). In preparing this list, be realistic about the amounts and timing of anticipated income. Remember, the cash-flow projection is *your* management tool. This is no time for rose-colored glasses. Once you've projected income, fill in the expense line items (disbursements) you know will be due.

We recommend that your projection be designed to cover at least the next three to six months, but preferably the next 12 months. As each month expires, the cash-flow projection needs to be updated based on that month's actual activities and any new information you have about future receipts and disbursements. Remember, the goal of cash forecasting is to anticipate and plan your press's inflow and outflow of cash so you'll always have enough money at the right time to pay your bills and keep the press in a stable situation.

Cash
Forecasting
Tips

Cash Forecasting Tips

- Be conservative when projecting cash receipts. Only include amounts you have a high degree of confidence in receiving. Don't overestimate!

- Make sure you include every amount you expect to pay. Don't leave any disbursements out.

- Know that many receipts and expenses will fluctuate from month to month. Don't list the same amounts for each month if you know they will vary.

- Use last year's activity as a guide in preparing the cash-flow projection.

Cash-Flow Projection

	July	Aug.	Sept.	Oct.	Nov.	Dec.	Jan.	Feb.	March	April	May	June	Total
CASH RECEIPTS													
Book Sales:													
Distributors													
Direct													
Contributions													
Confirmed													
Expected													
Government Grants:													
Confirmed													
Expected													
Special Events													
Loans Received													
Other Receipts													
Transfer from Investments													
Transfer from Restricted Funds													
Total Receipts													
CASH DISBURSEMENTS													
Book Production Expenses													
Operating Expenses													
Payments on Loans													
Other Disbursements													
Payment on Past Due Payables													
Transfer to Investments													
Total Disbursements													
Cash Excess (Short)													
Cash Beginning of Month													
Cash End of Month													

Note: Cash Receipts minus Disbursements equals Cash Excess/(Short). Cash Excess/(Short) plus Cash Beginning Month equals Ending Cash.

Figure 8-1
Cash-Flow Projection

Borrowing Money

Even with the best cash-flow forecasting, your press may come up short of cash several months of the year. This section is about borrowing money. But in a more basic sense it is about money and the strategic use of money. It is also about options. And for a cash-strapped small nonprofit press, knowing that financial options are available when dollars are tight may be just the ticket to providing transitional capital to stabilize monthly operations.

Before we go any further, let's clear up some myths about borrowing money.

- *"Borrowing money means I'm a bad manager."* The truth is, your business is all about inventory and receivables and you'd have to be incredibly well capitalized or a brilliant cash-flow balancer to not need to borrow money on occasion.

- *"Borrowing puts me in debt."* There's a difference between debt financing as a *financial strategy* and debt as a *state of being*! Whether your press has a negative cash-flow situation or a deficit situation is important to know in determining whether or not your press is a candidate for borrowing money. Lenders do not look kindly on and usually will not provide financing for a deficit situation unless a legitimate and viable plan for reversing the deficit is presented with the loan request—and even then, nothing is for sure. They are much more likely, however, to approve a loan to carry your press through a period of negative cash flow.

Good Reasons to Borrow Money

Aside from financing for equipment purchases and capital improvements, there are three primary situations in which your press should consider borrowing money:

- **For Short-Term Cash Flow**—In times of negative cash flow, your press might consider a "cash flow" or "bridge" loan, which is then paid off when the anticipated source of income, such as a grant or large receivable account, is subsequently received.

- **For Working Capital**—Accounts receivable and inventory are considered current assets of your press, but they are not easily converted to cash—especially inventory. Because of this they can take up a lot of the press's working capital, leaving very little in actual cash to pay current bills; they may even create a negative cash-flow situation. Lenders, however, often allow organizations to borrow against their working capital. Working-capital loans are similar in many ways to cash-flow loans, but are generally out for a longer period and are considered more risky.

  Working-capital loans are repaid from your press's general income stream. To obtain such a loan, you will need to show that your press, overall, is in positive financial condition, based on its cash-flow history and projected trends.

- **To Take Advantage of an Opportunity**—Good opportunities don't always wait for times when you have cash on hand. To benefit from such opportunities, your press might consider borrowing the money needed. A good example of such a situation is the need to do a second printing of a particular book. If the first printing outsold the original projections and all indications are that a second printing would do equally well, but there's no cash available for a second printing, an "opportunity" type loan may be in order. The terms of such a loan should state that any sales proceeds for that book must go first toward the loan and not for other expenses of the press.

Borrowing money is certainly not an option for all small nonprofit presses, and for those that it is, the key thing to remember is that it comes with strings attached. The longest string of all is that the loan not only has to be repaid, it must be repaid with interest.

Financing Resources

The most obvious source for your small press to seek a loan from is a bank or a traditional lender. Banks, however, are not always receptive to loan requests from nonprofit organizations because often these organization do not have a reliable source of collateral for securing the loan. Without adequate collateral, banks see such loans as presenting too great a risk.

But banks aren't the only lending source available. Examples of alternative lenders include foundation and community loan funds. If there is no foundation-sponsored or arts loan fund in your press's community, check with local foundations, particularly the community foundation in your town, and suggest they start such a fund for nonprofits in the area. More and more foundations are buying into this kind of activity.

The Best Time to Apply for a Loan

The best time for your press to request a loan is when it is in its *best* cash position. This demonstrates the press's ability to anticipate its upcoming cash-flow needs and gives both the loan officer and the press the time to fully understand and process the loan request.

There may be times, however, when your press's need for cash is more urgent. In these circumstances, having a firm understanding of your press's financial situation will put you on a better footing for negotiating a loan from a position of strength and help you avoid appearing desperate for money. Desperation carries an added risk for both the borrower and the lender—a risk that is usually better left not taken by each.

Knowing What to Present

When considering a loan request, most lending institutions will want to see the press's most recent audited financial statements, a current balance sheet, a current statement of activities with actual-to-budget comparisons and cash-flow projections. All of this information is important to the loan officer analyzing the loan request, but it is ultimately the cash-flow projection that indicates how much money is needed, over what period of time and how best the loan should be structured. The cash-flow projection also forecasts your press's ability to have enough cash after the loan is repaid to carry on effectively.

Be sure the loan officer understands your press's mission and programs, the market demand for its products and services and the benefit your press's work brings to the community or society. Clearly convey your dedication to the press's mission and your enthusiasm for your work. Your ability to effectively communicate this information may not persuade the lender to make the loan, but it will add credibility to your presentation.

Be aware that while conversing with you about the loan request, the loan officer will also be judging your management strength. In addition to objectively analyzing your press's financial statements, the loan officer is also responsible for assessing character. The more confident and knowledgeable you are in your presentation, especially regarding your press's financial situation, the more confidence the lender is likely to have in your ability to repay the loan.

The amount and purpose of each loan will determine how much information the lender will need to process your application. In general, however, you should be prepared to address the following six points:

- **Amount to be Borrowed**—This is the first thing the loan officer will want to know. It pays to do both good budgeting and cash forecasting before going to the bank.

- **Date the Loan is Needed**—Advanced planning goes a long way toward enhancing your management credibility. It also gives the loan officer the necessary time to get the loan approved, prepare loan documents, get the check signed and close the loan. Most lending institutions need at least one week from start to finish to accomplish all of these functions.

- **Use of the Loan**—Be prepared to tell the loan officer the purpose for which the funds will be used.

- **Suggested Repayment Schedule**—The repayment schedule can be structured in a variety of ways, including lump-sum payment at the end of the loan period, interest-only payments for a period of time or monthly installment payments of principal and interest. The best way to match the repayment schedule with your press's cash-flow projections is for *you* to suggest how this will be structured. If the cash-flow projections are prepared properly, this is the best way to guarantee that the loan will be repaid as promised.

- **Repayment Source**—The more explicit and reliable the source of repayment, the more likely your press is to get a loan. This is doubly true if you have an alternative source of repayment to offer as back up in the event that the first falls through.

- **Collateral or Guarantee**—Most traditional lenders (banks) are obligated by regulators to place safeguards on the loans they make through the use of collateral. Some alternative financing institutions will not require as much collateral as a bank, but some type of security will most likely be needed. Types of collateral your press might be asked to pledge are its capital assets (furniture and equipment), book inventory, accounts receivable or grants or contributions receivable. Another option is for the loan to be *guaranteed*. This means that another party, such as a foundation or individual members of the board, agrees in writing to repay the loan should the press default on its obligation.

Most lenders evaluate loan requests based on an organization's ability to repay the loan, its management strength and available collateral. Under the right circumstances, your press should consider borrowing money as a viable option for ensuring its financial stability.

chapter 9

Payroll, Performance and Policies

The Basics of Personnel Management

Chapter Highlights

▶ **Establishing a Personnel Filing System**

▶ **Payroll Administration**

▶ **Job Performance Tools**

▶ **Personnel Policies**

Payroll, Performance and Policies
The Basics of Personnel Management

Although your employees don't appear anywhere on the press's balance sheet, the fruits of their work produce both assets and liabilities for you as a nonprofit publisher. Finding the right blend of talented and dedicated employees is but the first challenge you'll face as a nonprofit manager. Once your staff is hired, you'll need to master the ins and outs of personnel management to minimize both the headaches and risks that go with the role of "employer."

An effective personnel system spells out employee job responsibilities, duties and performance expectations. It also sets up a reliable system of policies and procedures for you, the employer, as you make your way through the vagaries of personnel administration.

This chapter spells out the "3-Ps" of personnel administration—payroll, performance and personnel policies. But before getting into the technical, let's first get organized!

Establishing a Personnel Filing System

When a new employee is hired, you'll need a filing system for personnel-related information and to document future work history. Most office supply stores carry preprinted file sets, or "personnel jackets," for recording employee data in one central place. In addition to basic information like address, phone numbers and emergency contacts, these standard files have numerous other sections for tracking time off and other ongoing employment activities.

Whatever system you choose, be sure the contents of the file include at least the following documents:

- resumé;
- references provided at application;
- employment letter or agreement (if applicable);
- a completed IRS Form W-4;
- a completed I-9 Immigration Form (if applicable);

- job description;
- benefit enrollment forms;
- performance reviews;
- wage and salary actions and history;
- employee emergency data form; and
- vacation and sick leave tracking form.

When a staff member resigns, you'll add both a termination letter and a Consolidated Omnibus Budget Reconciliation Act (COBRA) form to the file, if you will continue to carry the separating employee's health insurance. COBRA permits former employees to continue health insurance through their previous employer, at their own expense, for up to 18 months after termination.

It goes without saying that personnel records should be kept in a safe, locked place with access limited to appropriate managerial staff. We also recommend you keep personnel files for a minimum of five years after employment separation.

Payroll Administration

Though few employees work in a nonprofit press for the money, most do rely on their biweekly or monthly paychecks to make ends meet. For their sake—and yours—mastering the art of payroll administration is a must.

The payroll function starts with the W-4 form each employee completes upon hiring. The W-4 is the IRS form that determines the amount of income tax employers will withhold and forward to the respective federal and state agencies on behalf of their employees. The IRS provides elaborate instructions to assist you and your new employee in determining the correct withholding allowance. From then on, it's your job to make sure the amounts withheld are submitted in a timely manner according to IRS "Circular E: Employer's Tax Guide" and your state's local equivalent. How often you make these tax deposits depends on the size of your payroll. The most valuable advice we can give you is to fully understand and comply with the amount and timing requirements established by your tax authority. If you don't, you may end up with interest and penalties that could threaten the financial viability of your press.

In addition to state and federal withholding taxes, employees must contribute a portion of each paycheck for Medicare and Social Security (FICA) taxes. As an employer, you are required to match both of these employee contributions, and, though your amount isn't large (7.65 percent at the time of this writing), this may turn out to be the only "retirement plan" you will ever be able to offer employees. So make that matching contribution with pride!

Figure 9-1

How Payroll is
Calculated

How Payroll is Calculated

$ Gross Wages
(-) $ Federal income tax
(-) $ Social Security tax (6.2% of gross wages)
(-) $ Medicare tax (1.45% of gross wages)
(-) $ State income tax
(-) $ Other employee deductions (if applicable)
$ Net wages (take home pay)

In addition to the tax deposits you will make on behalf of your employees, you are also required to file various quarterly and annual payroll tax reports to the appropriate federal and state authorities. These reports summarize and document your press's payroll activity, and also carry hefty penalties if not filed in a timely manner. Figure 9-2 describes most of the federal and local tax forms required of nonprofit employers. Check with your accountant or local authorities to be sure you're in compliance with all state and federal reporting requirements.

Figure 9-2

Required Federal and
State Tax Forms

Quarterly

IRS Form 941—A summary of all wages paid during the quarter, payroll taxes withheld, deposits made on those withheld taxes and a reconciliation of the amount still owed to the IRS or of a refund due your press.

Unemployment Quarterly Tax Report—Some states require quarterly reporting and payment for unemployment insurance tax. This is paid by the employer, not withheld from employee wages.

State Income Tax Form—If required, a summary of wages paid during the quarter, state income taxes withheld, deposits made on those withheld taxes and a reconciliation of the amount due the state or of a refund due your press for overpayment of taxes.

. . . .

Annually

IRS Form W-2—A statement of wages paid to each employee during the calendar year. This form is then used by the employee to prepare the individual income tax return. Besides providing each employee with a W-2, your press must also file a copy of all employees' W-2s with the Social Security Administration. The W-2s submitted to the Social Security Administration are accompanied by Form W-3, a transmittal form summarizing all of the information contained on the W-2s.

State Form—A statement that piggybacks on the annual payroll reporting procedures that the IRS requires. Accordingly, your press is required to submit a state copy of Form W-2 along with a report that summarizes the W-2 information to the appropriate state taxing agency.

State Unemployment Tax Form—A report that summarizes your contribution to the state's unemployment fund. Contributions are based on a percentage of wages paid during the period. In most states, this tax is only imposed on wages up to a specified amount for each employee. (Done quarterly in Minnesota, no annual summary for the state).

Because the payroll function can be time-consuming, complex and subject to frequently changing regulations, we strongly encourage small nonprofit employers to contract with a local payroll service to issue paychecks, make the tax deposits and file all payroll tax forms and reports. Most employers find the expenses of a payroll service to be money well spent. You lose the headaches of keeping up with all the regulations and gain valuable time for other management functions.

If you go the payroll service route though, be sure to do your homework in choosing the right vendor, especially if they will be making your tax deposits. You want to be sure the company is solvent and has an impeccable record in making timely and accurate deposits for their clients.

....

Job Performance Tools

Effective job performance starts with a clear and straightforward job description that outlines the employee's responsibilities and performance expectations. Even in presses where employees wear multiple hats, the job description is an important baseline for both employee and employer to know whether the job is getting done within performance expectations.

Job descriptions should include:

- the mission of the press;
- responsibilities and duties of the particular job;
- skills, experience, educational background and personal qualities necessary for the job;
- supervisory reporting relationships; and
- salary range for the position.

Employees' performance should be evaluated on at least an annual basis, with the job description providing the foundation for the appraisal. Some nonprofits evaluate new employees after the first three months of employment so course corrections can be suggested before incorrect habits can be established.

Again, office supply stores carry all-purpose performance appraisal forms. You can also use the job description to create your own employee evaluation form. Either way, employees need regular feedback on how they are performing. Whatever instrument you choose, give your employees a chance to complete the same form prior to the evaluation. This gives you both an opportunity to see if your views on performance are in sync.

Remember, the goal of the performance appraisal is to create a feedback loop that ensures the employee's success and productivity. So do yourself and your staff a favor by not saving up major negative feedback for the annual perform-ance appraisal. Employees deserve honest, straightforward feedback as situations occur. Employees rightly perceive the accumulation of negatives delivered only once a year as "dumping." Likewise, saving up compliments for once-a-year communication deprives the employee of recognition and you of opportunities to motivate and praise.

....

Personnel Policies

Once your nonprofit press has grown from a small collection of founding staff to a larger cadre of professionals, you'll move into "personnel policy territory." Well-constructed personnel policies are like an organizational rule book. They communicate what's expected of employees in a manner that is fair and applicable to all. Best of all, they relieve you, the employer, of coming up with individual responses to each employee requests—you, and they, now have a company guidebook for your decisions.

Personnel policies no doubt protect you as an employer. By spelling out the code of conduct and expectations that apply to all, you limit the potential for partiality, which may be inevitable with a growing staff. But personnel policies also protect the employee, and for that reason, we recommend that you seek legal advice as you draft your first set of policies.

These days, employment law is big business in all states. Luckily, your local attorney general's office is likely to have a free "employer's guide" spelling out specific personnel requirements within your state. This is a great place to start. Your colleagues in the publishing world or other nonprofits are also potential resources in the development phase of a personnel manual. Many nonprofits don't think twice about sharing their personnel manuals with colleagues—and though we applaud this generosity, the onus is still on you to be sure the policies you're duplicating are legal as well as applicable to you. Although the personnel manual will be specific to each press, you'll want to include the key components listed in Figure 9-3.

Figure 9-3
Elements of a Policy and Procedures Manual

Elements of a Policy and Procedures Manual

- Equal employment/affirmative action statements
- Vacation, sick and other leave policies
- Performance expectations and evaluation
- Employment status and termination policies
- Harassment policy
- Policy on alcohol and drug use

There's a lot more to personnel administration than we can cover in this handbook. We encourage you to master these fundamentals, and once implemented, to continue to look for opportunities to refine and improve your system. Just like any other function, personnel administration is as much art as science. But specific employment and tax laws require you to take your role as "employer" very seriously. When in doubt on any personnel issue, be it tax or legal, we urge you to seek competent counsel from your accountant or legal advisor.

On that note, we end the "advice" portion of this manual with hopes that the information presented contributes to the knowledge base and bottom line of your nonprofit press.

appendix
· · · · · · · · · · · · · · · ·

Accounting Worksheets

Contents

▶ **Total Book Budget**

▶ **Total Expense Budget by Department**

▶ **Department Expenses—Budget-to-Actual Comparison**

▶ **Monthly Budget**

▶ **Accounts Payable Register**

▶ **Accounts Payable Subsidiary Ledger and Aging**

▶ **Cash Disbursements Journal**

▶ **Direct Sales Register**

▶ **Cash Receipts Journal**

▶ **Accounts Receivable Subsidiary Ledger and Aging**

▶ **Perpetual Book Inventory Register (by book)**

▶ **Perpetual Book Inventory Register (all books)**

▶ **Payroll Register**

▶ **Sample General Journal**

▶ **General Journal**

Total Book Budget For Fiscal Year _____

Account Description	Book One	Book Two	Book Three	Book Four	Book Five	Book Six	Book Seven	Book Eight	Book Nine	Book Ten	Backlist	Total
EARNED INCOME												
Direct Sales												
Distributor Sales												
Wholesale Sales												
(Discounts)												
(Returns)												
(Returns Processing Fee)												
(Refunds)												
Subsidiary Rights Sales												
Projected Total Earned Income												
COST OF BOOKS SOLD												
1) Inventoriable Costs:												
Acquisition/Agent Fees												
Permission Fees												
Rights Payments												
Translation Fees												
Cover Design/Artwork												
Copyediting												
Proofreading												
Typesetting												
Paper, Printing & Binding												
Shipping (Manufacturing)												
Total Inventoriable Costs												
2) NonInventoriable Costs												
Royalty Expense												
Distribution Fees												
Total NonInventoriable Costs												
Projected Total Cost of Books Sold												
Projected Gross Profit												

Total Expense Budget
by Department

For Fiscal Year _____

Account Description	Production	Editorial	Marketing and Promotion	Fund-Raising	Management and General	Total
Salaries						
Payroll Taxes						
Employee Benefits						
Professional Fees						
Outside Editorial Services						
Supplies						
Telephone						
Postage and Shipping						
Occupancy						
Equipment Rental and Maintenance						
Insurance						
Travel						
Trade Show Expense						
Advertising and Promotions						
Catalog Expense						
Review Copies						
Other Fund-Raising Expense						
Employee Training Conferences and Conventions						
Special Event Expenses						
Interest Expense						
Dues and Subscriptions						
Bank Charges						
Miscellaneous						
Amortization						
Depreciation						
Total Operating Expenses						

Name of Press
Department Expenses—Budget-to-Actual Comparison
For the Six Months Ended _____, _____
Department: _____

	Current Month			Year-To-Date			Annual Budget
	Actual	**Budget**	**Variance**	**Actual**	**Budget**	**Variance**	**Budget**
Operating Expenses							
Salaries							
Payroll Taxes							
Employee Benefits							
Professional Fees							
Outside Editorial Services							
Supplies							
Telephone							
Postage and Shipping							
Occupancy							
Equipment Rental and Maintenance							
Insurance							
Travel							
Trade Show Expense							
Advertising and Promotions							
Review Copies							
Catalog Expense							
Other Fund-Raising Expense							
Employee Training							
Conferences and Conventions							
Special Event Expenses							
Interest Expense							
Dues and Subscriptions							
Bank Charges							
Miscellaneous							
Amortization							
Depreciation							
Total Operating Expenses							

Monthly Budget For Fiscal Year _____

	July	Aug.	Sept.	Oct.	Nov.	Dec.	Jan.	Feb.	March	April	May	June	Total
Book Income													
Direct Sales													
Distributor Sales													
Wholesale Sales													
(Discounts)													
(Sales Returns)													
(Returns Processing Fees)													
(Refunds)													
Net Sales													
Subsidiary Rights Income													
Total Book Income													
Cost of Books Sold													
Inventory Beginning of Year													
Acquisition/Agent Fees													
Permission Fees													
Rights Payments													
Translation Fees													
Cover Design/Artwork													
Copyediting													
Proofreading													
Typesetting													
Paper, Printing & Binding													
Shipping													
Obsolete Inventory Adjust.													
Cost of Books Available for Sale													
Less: Inventory End of Year													
Total Production Costs													
Royalty Expense													
Distribution Fees													
Total Cost of Books Sold													
Gross Profit													

continued

continued

Monthly Budget For Fiscal Year

	July	Aug.	Sept.	Oct.	Nov.	Dec.	Jan.	Feb.	March	April	May	June	Total
Operating Expenses													
Salaries													
Payroll Taxes													
Employee Benefits													
Professional Fees													
Outside Editorial Services													
Supplies													
Telephone													
Postage and Shipping													
Occupancy													
Equip. Rental and Maint.													
Insurance													
Travel													
Trade Show Expense													
Advertising and Promotions													
Review Copies													
Catalog Expense													
Other Fund-Raising Expense													
Employee Training													
Conferences & Conventions													
Interest Expense													
Dues and Subscriptions													
Bank Charges													
Miscellaneous													
Amortization													
Depreciation													
Total Operating Expenses													
(Loss from Operations)													
Support & Other Income													
Foundation Grants													
Corporate Grants													
Government Grants													
Individual Contributions													
Board Support													
Sponsorships													
In-Kind Contributions													
Special Events Income													
(Special Event Expenses)													
Interest Income													
Other Income													
Total Support/Other Income													
Surplus (Deficit)													

Accounts Payable Register

Date	Vendor/Creditor	Vendor Account Code	Invoice Date	Invoice Number	Invoice Amount	Expense Account Name	Expense Account #	Expense Account Amount	Date Paid	Amount Paid	Check#
Monthly Totals											

Accounts Payable Subsidiary Ledger and Aging

Acct. #	Vendor/Creditor	Invoice Date	Total Amount Due	0-30 days	31-60 Days	61-90 days	Over 90 days	
	Total All Vendors							

Cash Disbursements Journal

Date	Payee	Check #	Amount					
	Total for Month							

Direct Sales Register

Inv. Date	Customer Name	Customer #	Invoice #	Invoice Amount	Income Account Number	Title/ Book ID	Type of Book*	Customer Type+
	Monthly Totals							

*Type of Book:
P—Paperback
H—Hardcover

+Customer Type:
L—Library
W—Wholesaler

I—Individual
C—Classroom

B—Bookstore

Cash Receipts Journal

Date	Received From	Customer #	Invoice #	Accounts Receivable Amount	Non-accounts Receivable Amount	Income Acct. Code if Non-Accts. Receivable	
	Monthly Totals						

Accounts Receivable Subsidiary Ledger and Aging

Customer ID#	Customer Name/Invoice #	Invoice Date	Total Amount Due	0-30 days	31-60 days	61-90 days	Over 90 days	
	Total All Customers							

Perpetual Book Inventory Register (by book)

Title:	Publication Date:	Books Printed:	
Author:	ISBN#:	Total Cost:	Unit Cost:

Date	Transaction Description*	Units	Dollars					
			Debit	Credit	Balance			
Total All Vendors								

*Transaction Descriptions:
- Sales
- Returns
- Inventory Adjustment
- Damaged (Hurts)
- Books to Authors
- Review Copies

Perpetual Book Inventory Register (all books)

Title/Author	Book Code	Beginning of Year		Added to Inventory		Sold/Issued		Returns		End of Year	
		Units	Cost	Units	Cost	Units	Cost	Units	Cost	Units	Cost
Totals											

Payroll Register

For Payroll Period Ending: _____, _____

Employee ID#	Employee/ Department	Gross Wages	Social Security Withholding	Medicare Withholding	Federal Income Tax Withholding	State Income Tax Withholding	Retirement Benefits Withholding	Medical Benefits Withholding	Other Withholding	Net Pay	Check #	Check Date
Totals for Pay Period												

Sample General Journal

	For the Month of _____ , _____				

General Journal Entry #	Account Description	Account #	Amount		
			Debit	Credit	
GJO701	Depreciation Expense				
	Accumulated Depreciation				
	To record depreciation expense for _____, _____				
GJO702	Cost of Books Sold				
	Change in Inventory				
	To record Cost of Books Sold in _____, _____				
GJO703	Bank Charge Expense				
	Cash—Checking				
	To record bank charges for _____, _____				
GJO704	Cash—Savings				
	Investments				
	Interest Income				
	To record interest for _____, _____				
GJO705	Grants Receivable				
	Income Foundation Grants				
	To record grant receivable				
GJO706	Cash—Savings				
	Cash—Checking				
	To record a cash transfer from checking to savings				

General Journal

For the Month of _____ , _____

General Journal Entry #	Account Description	Account #	Amount Debit	Credit	

glossary

Terms Used in Nonprofit Accounting

Account—A record of an organization's financial transactions maintained in a special book or ledger. Separate accounts are kept for assets, liabilities, net assets, revenues and expenses.

Account Number—An assigned number which provides numerical control over accounts and provides a convenient means of referring to the account.

Accounting Period—The period of time for which an operating statement is customarily prepared. Examples: a month (the most common accounting period), four weeks, a quarter (of a year), 26 weeks, a year, 52 weeks.

Accounting System—A network of procedures through which financial transactions and information are accumulated, classified in the accounts, recorded in the various books of account and reported in the financial statements.

Accounts Payable—A liability representing the amount owed to others for merchandise or services provided to the organization.

Accounts Receivable—An asset representing the amounts owed to the organization.

Accessions—Additions, both purchased and donated, to collections held by museums, art galleries, botanical gardens, libraries and similar entities.

Accrual Basis Accounting—An accounting system that recognizes expenses when they are incurred and revenues when they are earned, rather than when cash changes hands. It records amounts payable and amounts receivable in addition to recording transactions resulting from the exchange of cash.

Adjusting (Journal) Entry—The record made of an accounting transaction giving effect to the correction of an error, an accrual, a write-off, a provision for bad debts or depreciation, or the like.

Compiled by The Stevens Group with acknowledgement to the Public Management Institute and the Financial Accounting Standards Board.

Administrative Budget—A financial plan under which an organization carries on its day-to-day affairs under the common forms of administrative management; a budget. The term is usually employed in contradistinction to capital budget or program budget, where the plan covers transactions of a non-operating character.

Agency Fund—*See Custodian Funds.*

Allocate—To charge an item or group of items of revenue or cost to one or more objects, activities, processes, operations or products, in accordance with cost responsibilities, benefits received or other readily identifiable measure of application or consumption.

Annuity Gift—A gift whereby money or other property is given to an organization on the condition that the organization bind itself to pay periodically to the donor or other designated individuals stipulated amounts, which payments are to terminate at a specified time.

Asset—A resource, object, or right of measurable financial value (e.g., cash, securities, accounts receivable, land, building and equipment).

Audit—A series of procedures followed by a professional accountant to test, on a selective basis, transactions and internal controls in effect, all with a view to forming an opinion on the fairness of the organization's annual financial statements.

Auxiliary Activity—An activity that furnishes a service that is not part of the basic program services of the organization. A fee is normally charged that is directly related, although not necessarily equal, to the cost of the service.

Balance Sheet—The financial statement that presents the financial position at a certain specified date. It lists assets, liabilities and net assets. May also be referred to as the Statement of Position.

Balanced Budget—A budget in which forward expenditures for a given period are matched by expected revenues for the same period.

Board-Designated Net Assets—A designation that is self-imposed by the board on a certain segment of its unrestricted net assets for some specific activity or project that is to be carried out in the future. Board-designation has no legal significance.

Budget—A financial plan which estimates the monetary receipts and expenditures for an operating period. Budgets may be directed toward project or program activities and are primarily used as a comparison and control feature against the actual financial results.

Capital Additions—Gifts, grants, bequests, investment income and gains on investments, restricted either permanently or for a period of time by parties outside of the organization to endowment and loan funds. Such additions also include similar resources restricted for fixed asset additions, but only to the extent expended during the year.

Capitalizing an Asset—The process of recording the cost of land, buildings, or equipment as fixed assets, rather than expensing them when they were initially acquired.

Cash Basis Accounting—An accounting system that records only those events that involve the exchange of cash and ignores transactions that do not involve cash.

Cash-Disbursements Journal—The journal recording all financial transactions involving the disbursement of cash.

Cash-Flow Statement—A statement of cash income and outgo between two given dates.

Cash Receipts Journal—The journal recording financial transactions involving the receipt of cash.

Certified Public Accountant (CPA)—An accountant licensed by the state to certify financial statements.

Chart of Accounts—A list that organizes the agency's accounts in a systematic manner, usually by account number, to facilitate the preparation of financial statements and periodic financial reports.

Coding Structure—A systematic formula for assigning account numbers to accounts.

Collections—Works of art, botanical and animal specimens, books and other items held for display or study by museums and similar institutions.

Comparative Statements—Balance sheets, income or flow statements, or other accounting summaries juxtaposed for the purpose of contrasting the financial characteristics of an organization from one period to another.

Conditional Promise to Give—A written or oral agreement to contribute cash or other assets to another entity in which the contribution depends on the occurrence of a specified future or uncertain event to bind the promisor.

Contributed Services—Contributed services are recognized as revenue only if they create or add value to a nonfinancial asset such as capital improvements to a building or office space; or if they require specialized skills that would typically need to be purchased if not provided by donation. Organizations recognizing contributed services are required to disclose a description of the service received by program or activity, nature and extent of the services, and the amount recognized as revenues.

Contribution—A transfer of cash or other assets to another entity in which the transfer is unconditional, made or received voluntarily, and is nonreciprocal.

Cost Center—An organizational division, department, or unit having common supervision.

Custodian Funds—Funds received and held by an organization as fiscal agent for others. Syn: Agency Funds.

De-accessions—Disposition of items in collections held by museums, art galleries, botanical gardens, libraries and similar entities resulting from sales or disposals.

Debit and Credit—Technical bookkeeping terms referring to the two sides of a financial occurrence. The increase or decrease effect on the account depends on the type of account. The debits must equal the credits for any given financial occurrence.

Deferred Revenue—Revenue received before it is earned. (For example, advance ticket sales or membership dues.)

Deficit—1. Expenses and losses in excess of related income; an operating loss. 2. An accumulation of operating losses ("negative" retained income).

Depreciating an Asset—The process by which the cost of a fixed asset is expensed over its useful life. The annual charge to expense is referred to as depreciation expense.

Designated Net Assets—Unrestricted net assets set aside by action of the governing board for specific purposes. See also Quasi-Endowment Funds, Board-Designated Net Assets.

Double-Entry Accounting—A method of bookkeeping that recognizes a two-way, self-balancing, debit/credit entry for all financial occurrences.

Encumbrances—Commitments in the form of orders, contracts, and similar items that will become payable when goods are delivered or services rendered.

Endowment—A type of donor restriction on contributed assets that stipulates that the assets endowed must remain intact either temporarily (until a stated period of time has passed or a specific occurrence has taken place) or permanently. The revenue earned from such assets is unrestricted unless specified otherwise by the donor or state law.

Exchange Transaction—A reciprocal transfer of assets in which the resource provider receives equal or commensurate value in exchange for the transferred assets.

Expendable Fund—A fund that is available to finance an organization's program and supporting services, including both unrestricted and restricted amounts.

Expenditure—The incurring of a liability, the payment of cash, or the transfer of property for the purpose of acquiring an asset or service or settling a loss.

Expense—Asset expended resulting in a decrease in the net assets.

FASB—FASB, the Financial Accounting Standards Board, is the governing board that formulates authoritative accounting standards for nongovernmental agencies. These standards, which encompass accounting rules, procedures, and applications, define accepted accounting practice and are referred to as Generally Accepted Accounting Principles (GAAP).

Fixed Asset—An asset that has a relatively long useful life, usually several years or more, such as land, building and equipment.

Functional Classification—A classification of expenses that accumulates expenses according to the purpose for which costs are incurred. The primary functional classifications are program and supporting services.

Fund—An accounting entity established for the purpose of accounting for resources used for specific activities or objectives in accordance with special purposes as restricted by a donor or as designated by the organization. Each organization can choose to account by funds based on its own needs to track specific financial activity.

Fund Accounting—An accounting system that divides the accounts into separate groupings that reflect various organizational or donor-restricted purposes and that indicate how assets were utilized for these specified purposes.

Fund Group—A group of funds of similar character, for example operating funds, endowment funds and annuity and life income funds.

Funds Held in Trust by Others—Resources held and administered, at the direction of the donor, by an outside trustee for the benefit of the organization.

GAAP—*See Generally Accepted Accounting Principles and FASB.*

General Journal—The book in which all financial transactions not involving the receipt or the disbursement of cash at the time of the occurrence are recorded.

General Ledger—The book of "final entry" which lists the organization's accounts, used for collecting financial information, by account, as it is posted from various journals.

Generally Accepted Accounting Principles—Accounting standards for nongovernmental agencies which encompass accounting rules, procedures and applications, and define accepted accounting practice. *See also FASB.*

Grant—An unconditional promise to give assets to an organization made by an individual or another organization. Grants must be recognized in the year the unconditional promise to give is received. *See also Multi-Year Grants.*

Guarantor—One who promises to make good if another fails to pay or otherwise perform an assigned or contractual task.

Income—Assets received resulting in an increase in the net assets.

Increase (Decrease) in Net Assets—The difference between "Total Revenue" and "Total Expenses" representing net financial results of operations for the period.

Interfund Receivable (Payable)—An amount that is due from one fund to another.

Interfund Transaction/Transfer—A transfer of assets from one fund to another.

Internal Control—The plan of organization, procedures and records designed to enhance the safeguarding of assets and the reliability of records of an organization.

Inventory—An asset consisting of goods purchased or produced and held for resale.

Investment Pool—Assets of several funds pooled or consolidated for investment purposes.

Investment Revenue—The revenue derived from the investment of assets. It includes interest, dividends and realized and unrealized capital gains (net of losses).

Journal—A book of original entry in which all financial transactions are initially recorded. All journal entries are subsequently posted to individual accounts in the ledger.

Journal Entry—An item in or prepared for a book of original entry, interpreting a business transaction in bookkeeping terms and showing the accounts to be debited and credited, together with an explanatory description of the transaction.

Liability—A claim on the assets by an outsider representing a financial obligation. Liabilities include accounts payable, accrued expenses and loans.

Life Annuity Agreement—An agreement whereby money or other property is given to an organization on the condition that the organization bind itself to pay periodically to the donor or other designated individual the income earned by the assets donated to the organization for the lifetime of the donor or of the designated individual.

Liquid Asset—Cash in banks and on hand, and other cash assets not set aside for specific purposes other than the payment of a current liability, or a readily marketable investment.

Market Value—The realizable amount for which an asset can be sold in the open market.

Modified Cash-Basis Accounting—The same as cash-basis accounting except for certain items which are treated on an accrual basis (e.g., depreciation and payroll taxes). This is also known as a "hybrid method."

Multi-Year Grant—An unconditional promise to give grant assets to an organization made by an individual or another organization, that extends beyond one year. These grants must be recognized in the year the unconditional promise to give is received and must be recorded using a discount rate to measure the present value of the estimated future cash flow.

Net Assets—The difference between the total assets (what is owned) and total liabilities (what is owed).

Net Investment in Plant—The total carrying value of all property, plant and equipment, and related liabilities, exclusive of real properties held for investment.

Nonexpendable Additions—*See Capital Additions.*

Object Classification of Expenses—A method of classifying expenditures according to their natural classification, such as salaries and wages, employee benefits, supplies, purchased services and so forth.

Operating Reserve—An unrestricted net asset used to stabilize an organization's finances.

Permanent Restriction—A donor-imposed restriction on a contribution that stipulates that the contributed assets be maintained permanently. Unless otherwise stipulated by the donor or state law, the organization is permitted to use up or expend part or all of the income derived from permanently restricted assets.

Pledge—A receivable representing a specified sum that an individual or organization has promised to contribute.

Posting—The process of recording in the appropriate accounts in the general ledger, summarized figures of the amounts that were recorded during the month in the books of the original entry, the journals.

Program Services—The programs and activities that represent the principle reason for the organization's existence.

Promise to Give—A promise to give is a written or oral agreement to contribute cash or other assets to another entity. A promise to give must contain sufficient verifiable documentation that a promise was made and received.

Property, Plant & Equipment Funds—A fund group that may contain all fixed assets as well as the assets that are donor-restricted or board-designated for the purpose of purchasing fixed assets.

Prospectus—A selling document used for fund-raising. A summary description of an organization's goals, needs, history, financial information and personnel.

Quasi-Endowment Funds—Unrestricted funds which the governing board of an organization, rather than a donor, has determined are to be retained and invested. The governing board has the right to decide at any time to expend the principal of such funds. *See Designated Funds, Board-Designated Funds.*

Refundable Advance—An asset which is transferred to an organization before a condition has been substantially met. Refundable advances are recorded as a liability on the balance sheet until conditions are met, at which time they are recognized as revenue.

Restricted Asset—An asset that has legal restrictions imposed on its use by the original donor.

Revenue—Assets earned or income from services performed or goods sold.

Statement of Activities—The financial statement that summarizes the financial activity for a given period of time. It presents the income, expenses and changes in net assets for the period.

Statement of Cash Flows—The financial statement which provides relevant information about the cash receipts and cash payments of an organization during a period.

Statement of Functional Expenses—The financial statement that details the specific types of expenses by object (i.e., rent, salaries, etc.) that were incurred in each of the programs and supporting activities delineated on the Statement of Activities.

Support—Income from voluntary contributions and grants.

Support Services—Auxiliary activities that provide the various support functions essential to achieve program services.

Temporary Restriction—A donor-imposed restriction on contributed assets which will eventually either expire with the passage of time or will be fulfilled through an action of the organization.

Trial Balance—A schedule listing all the accounts in the general ledger along with the debit or credit balance in each account to determine whether the total debits of all accounts equal the total credits.

Unconditional Promise to Give—A "no strings attached" written or oral agreement to contribute cash or other assets to another entity.

Unrealized Gain (or Loss)—The amount by which the market value of an asset exceeds (or is less than) the original cost of that asset.

Unrestricted Asset—An asset that has no legal restrictions placed on its use by the original donor; it can be used in carrying on operations in any manner decided upon.

Unrestricted Net Assets—Sometimes called operating funds or general funds, this net asset group contains the assets on which there are no donor restrictions and from which the bulk of financial activity is usually handled.

index

About the Authors

The Stevens Group specializes in financial and management services for tomorrow's nonprofits and foundations. Founded in 1982, The Stevens Group has brought capacity, results and strategies to hundreds of nonprofits and philanthropies through our consulting, loan fund and professional development services.

In 1990, The Andrew W. Mellon Foundation retained The Stevens Group to design and operate the Small Press Loan and Technical Assistance Program targeted at improving the capacity of nine leading nonprofit presses. This manual is one of the several products of that program. It is our gift to the field and a legacy to a program whose effect, we hope, will be lasting.

If you would like more information on the material contained in this handbook, or on The Stevens Group, please contact one of its three authors: Susan Kenny Stevens, Lisa M. Anderson or Eric P. Stoebner, CPA.